TRULY HOME

You Had Me at Merlot by Melissa Brayden. Leighton and Jamie have all the ingredients to turn their attraction into love, but it's a recipe for disaster.(978-1-63679-543-0)

Appalachian Awakening by Nance Sparks. The more Amber's and Leslie's paths cross, the more this hike of a lifetime begins to look like a love of a lifetime. (978-1-63679-527-0)

Dreamer by Kris Bryant. When life seems to be too good to be true and love is within reach, Sawyer and Macey discover the truth about the town of Ladybug Junction, and the cold light of reality tests the hearts of these dreamers. (978-1-63679-378-8)

Eyes on Her by Eden Darry. When increasingly violent acts of sabotage threaten to derail the opening of her glamping business, Callie Pope is sure her ex, Jules, has something to do with it. But Jules is dead…isn't she? (978-1-63679-214-9)

Letters from Sarah by Joy Argento. A simple mistake brought them together, but Sarah must release past love to create a future with Lindsey she never dreamed possible. (978-1-63679-509-6)

Lost in the Wild by Kadyan. When their plane crash-lands, Allison and Mike face hunger, cold, a terrifying encounter with a bear, and feelings for each other neither expects. (978-1-63679-545-4)

Not Just Friends by Jordan Meadows. A tragedy leaves Jen struggling to figure out who she is and what is important to her. (978-1-63679-517-1)

Of Auras and Shadows by Jennifer Karter. Eryn and Rina's unexpected love may be exactly what the Community needs to heal the rot that comes not from the fetid Dark Lands that surround the Community but from within. (978-1-63679-541-6)

The Secret Duchess by Jane Walsh. A determined widow defies a duke and falls in love with a fashionable spinster in a fight for her rightful home. (978-1-63679-519-5)

Winter's Spell by Ursula Klein. When former college roommates reunite at a wedding in Provincetown, sparks fly, but can they find true love when evil sirens and trickster mermaids get in the way? (978-1-63679-503-4)

Praise for the Truly series

Truly Wanted

"*Truly Wanted* by J.J. Hale is a friends-to-lovers romance about overcoming your fear to have the happiness you want and need...There is a lot of back-and-forth emotionally for the women, as they continue to weigh the pros and cons of romance. Not once, though, was there a moment of indecision about how much they love each other, and that was great."
—*Lesbian Review*

"A solid debut novel with a neurodivergent MC."—*Lez Review Books*

"*Truly Wanted* is a great read and full of heart. There's amazing secondary characters (can Ruby and Dani kiss please), real life struggles we all go through, and a quick trip to see the Spice Girls! Like, what else do you want in a book? I'm looking forward to what comes next from J.J. Hale!"—*Reeg Reads*

Truly Enough

"Such a beautiful story about acceptance and finding peace with your fears and worries."—*LESBIReviewed*

By the Author

Truly Wanted

Truly Enough

Truly Home

Visit us at www.boldstrokesbooks.com

TRULY HOME

by

J.J. Hale

2024

TRULY HOME

ISBN 13: 978-1-63679-579-9

This Trade Paperback Original Is Published By
Bold Strokes Books, Inc.
P.O. Box 249
Valley Falls, NY 12185

First Edition: March 2024

CREDITS
Editor: Jenny Harmon
Production Design: Stacia Seaman
Cover Design by Tammy Seidick

Acknowledgments

I love reading acknowledgments in books and seeing the different ways that authors write them. I love the glimpse it gives into an author's world and the many people involved in getting a story out there in so many different ways. However, being on the other side of it and trying to write those acknowledgments is a harder task to undertake! I'm three books in now, and I feel like there are never the right words to truly encapsulate my gratitude to anyone and everyone who has played a hand in getting my stories out into the world.

As always, to my family. The ones who give me the space, time, and motivation (and sometimes a kick up the ass) to get words out of my brain and onto a page. And the ones who give me plenty of inspiration for the characters that I write.

To the new friends I've made along the way, both authors and readers, especially the ones who took the time to read my stories and share their thoughts. Special shout-out to Jayne Hellier for beta reading this and giving me invaluable feedback.

To the whole team at Bold Strokes Books who work so much magic behind the scenes. Especially my editor, Jenny, whose encouraging comments keep me going through the editing process (especially the LOLs, my favourite!)

Lastly, to everyone who has reached out to me to let me know that my stories made you feel understood. Hearing so many people tell me how reading characters with ADHD, or seeing an author with ADHD publish books has been important to you means more than I can ever say.

To the people who showed me what home truly feels like.

PROLOGUE

A re you all right?"
Six-year-old Ruth Miller looked up into the greenest eyes she had ever seen. She wasn't sure she had ever known someone with green eyes in real life before now. She quickly wiped at her tear-streaked cheeks as the other girl continued talking.

"You're new, I've never seen you before. It's okay to be sad, lots of people are sad in here. Do you wanna talk about it?"

Ruth shook her head quickly. How could she talk when she didn't even know what to say? The past few days had been filled with so many new people asking her questions, and it was easier to say nothing at all than try to find the answers they seemed to want.

"Okay, let's play, then!"

The girl smiled and grabbed Ruth's hand, pulling her toward the centre of the big, bright room filled with toys. Instead of flinching back from the contact, Ruth surprised herself by closing her grip around the warm hand. She had never been comfortable with people she didn't know touching her, and she'd had far too much of it happening recently. Her life had become filled with nothing but unwelcome strangers, but in that moment, she was pretty sure she would follow the girl with the long brown hair and sparkling green eyes anywhere.

It had been less than a week since she woke up in the children's ward of the hospital and her life had changed forever. She hadn't spoken a word since that first day, when she called out for her mom. A lady with a strange smile and sad eyes had come to tell her that her mom and dad were gone. She didn't understand where they went but she was too afraid to ask.

The lady had asked her if she remembered anything, and she just shook her head no. She continued to shake her head even when flashes came back or she woke in the middle of the night coughing and thought she was back in the house that was getting so hot. Ruth heard them talking about a fire and about how lucky she was. She didn't feel so lucky in the big bed with so many strangers talking around her like she couldn't hear them.

After a couple of days, they said her aunt was coming, and everything would be okay. Ruth didn't even know that she had an aunt, and her throat hurt badly, so it was not okay. They all got worried because she wasn't eating, but she couldn't find the words to tell them why. They gave her cold food for her throat, but it was lumpy and smelled bad. Her dad made nice food the way she liked, so she would wait until he got back. She remembered being very sleepy. Her eyes would close a lot, and every time they opened, there was a different adult standing next to her.

Then one morning her eyes opened, and she got super excited because her mom was there. But as she blinked the sleep from her eyelids and the woman got closer, she realized it wasn't her mom. Her hair was longer, her eyes weren't sparkly blue like her mom's, and her face wasn't as round. Tears started to stream down her face as the woman introduced herself as her Aunt Greta, her mom's sister.

Greta gave her nicer food at least. It wasn't as good as her dad's, but her stomach hurt, and she wanted to eat it so they would all stop staring at her. Greta didn't ask lots of questions, which was good. It wasn't that Ruth was choosing not to talk, she just didn't know what to say or how to say it. Greta read her some books, and they watched cartoons together, and then she'd brought Ruth to the big, bright room. It was the first time Ruth had left the room she had woken up in, and it was strange to see other people her age in other rooms as they passed. The world was still going even though it was all so different now.

Greta had tried getting her to play with some toys, but Ruth sat in the corner and watched the lights change colour on the ceiling. That's when the girl with green eyes had come in, and Ruth couldn't help her eyes darting toward her. Now here she was, sitting in the middle of the room as the girl sorted through the toy boxes like she knew exactly what she was looking for.

"So, what's your name anyway?"

Ruth blinked and turned her attention back to the girl as she dumped a box of LEGO on the floor between them and started to put pieces together. Her brain struggled to find the words. She knew her name, of course she did, so why couldn't she say it? Tears welled again until the girl spoke.

"It's okay if you can't talk. We can still be friends. My name is Livvie and I'm nine. Everybody says I talk a lot anyway, so I can talk enough for the both of us."

Ruth's tears subsided, and for the first time since she woke up in the hospital bed, a sense of calm surrounded her. Looking at Livvie happily building beside her, the ghost of a smile made its way onto her face. Livvie grinned at her and nodded toward the beginning of a house. Ruth took it as an invitation for her to contribute to its construction and was glad Livvie wasn't demanding words in return.

Despite the lack of reciprocated conversation, Livvie took Ruth under her wing. When Ruth had to return to her room, a pang of sadness washed over her until Livvie cocked her head to the side and said, "Same time tomorrow?"

Ruth looked hopefully toward Greta, who smiled and nodded. A tear slid down Greta's cheek and she wiped it away quickly before she held out a hand and said, "Let's go, Roo." The nickname brought tears of her own to Ruth's eyes and reminded her of her parents. The thought made her remember all over again that they weren't there. When would she get to go home?

Sure as her word, the next day Livvie met her in the same place, and they continued the LEGO house that sat untouched as if it was waiting for them to come back. Ruth had so many questions for Livvie but still couldn't find the words to ask them. Why was she there? She didn't look sick, and hospitals were for sick people, right? As if Livvie could read her mind, she slowly started to answer most of the questions that never left Ruth's lips while filling the silence as they played.

"My little sister Gracie is the sick one, not me. We come here a lot. This time has been long. I go to school and then I come here after and play while Mom stays with Gracie and talks to the doctor. My favourite is Dr Sutton, he sometimes brings me stickers and lets me help out with stuff. Is he your doctor, too?"

Ruth shrugged. Truthfully, she had no idea who her doctor was. She knew what they looked like, but they said so many things she couldn't remember them all.

"He's taller than anyone else in the room and he wears glasses and kinda looks like Superman when he's not Superman, ya know? My mom says so."

Ruth shook her head. Superman was definitely not her doctor, that's for sure. Her doctor was older than her dad and always wore a tie that had animals on it. She had gotten into the habit of counting the animals on the tie while the doctor talked to her aunt.

The next few days all followed the same pattern. Ruth would wait until it was close enough to the time Livvie would arrive. Then Greta would bring her to the playroom, and they would work on the brick house. Livvie would talk, Ruth would listen, and the heavy knot in her tummy would loosen a little. Livvie was like…the times she got extra marshmallows on a hot chocolate, or those chocolate chips she loved finding in her ice cream. Surprise goodness, her mom would call it. They would look for surprise goodness every day together and point it out. Her mom said it was important to savour all the goodness they could find.

It was about a week after she first met Livvie, maybe more, Ruth wasn't really sure anymore. They were so close to finishing the outside of the house, and they had even made some furniture to go inside. Livvie made a super cool couch, and she showed Ruth how to make it look so real. Greta crouched beside them, and Ruth glanced up, hoping her time with Livvie wasn't over already.

"I'm going to go grab some sandwiches downstairs so we don't have to eat the hospital food again. I'll let the nurses know so they'll keep an eye out if you need anything. Will you be okay here for a few minutes?"

Livvie piped up before Ruth had a chance and answered for her.

"I'll take care of her. I'm good at that. I take care of my sister lots when my mom gets food and showers and stuff."

Greta smiled that sad smile Ruth had seen aimed at her too often. She didn't see why Greta was sad about anything Livvie said. It sounded perfect to her.

"Thanks, honey. I'll be back soon, Roo."

Ruth was already back to building. Their house was looking pretty cool already and she was excited to finish it.

"So, your name is Roo? Like the kangaroo from Winnie-the-Pooh? That's kinda cool."

Ruth opened and closed her mouth before nodding slowly at Livvie. Roo would be good enough for now. It was a little reminder from her real life, but different, too. Just like everything else was in here. Livvie leaned in before glancing to the right and left like she was holding the biggest secret behind her lips. She whispered so softly Ruth had to strain to hear her.

"Okay, Roo, time for an adventure through the Hundred Acre Wood."

Ruth followed Livvie from the room. She was sure her aunt wouldn't want her to leave, but she also wouldn't want her alone, right? Plus, Livvie knew where they were going. They passed some of the rooms Ruth recalled on the way there, and Livvie waved through most of the windows. Kids, parents, and even nurses waved back. It was like everyone knew her, and Ruth followed her in awe. They ducked around a corner and Ruth's heart began to race. It was darker down there, quieter than the rest of the ward.

"These rooms are usually empty after therapies are done. They'll be perfect."

For what? Ruth's mind screamed, but the words stayed trapped. The longer she couldn't get them out, the harder it became. Livvie was good at knowing what Ruth wanted to say even when she couldn't say it, though, so she answered anyway.

"Time for hide and seek," Livvie said. Her eyes gleamed with a contagious excitement before she turned to cover her eyes and count.

Ruth glanced around quickly for somewhere to hide and

spotted some bean bags in the corner. She needed to hide quietly enough not to give her place away, so she tiptoed over and crept beneath the pile. The weight of the bean bags on top of her felt good, and she relaxed as she waited for Livvie to find her. It didn't take long for the bean bag to move and Livvie's smiling face to appear above Ruth.

"Gotcha! Your turn!"

Livvie was gone before Ruth even had her eyes closed. She began counting in her head and tried to ignore the worry that her aunt would be mad if she returned before they got back to the bright room. Ruth found Livvie quicker than she expected, and the excitement of the game soon pushed the worries from her mind.

"Ready or not, here I come!" Livvie whisper-yelled.

Ruth stifled a giggle from her hiding place. She was proud of it. It was hard to find anywhere good to hide in the small rooms. The only help she had was the dim lighting and quiet. Ruth tracked the sounds Livvie made as she searched. Livvie was humming an unfamiliar tune along the way. It was never quite silent with Livvie around, and Ruth was grateful for that. She held her breath so she wouldn't make a sound as the footsteps got closer.

Ruth was crouched inside a closet filled with soft mats that left little room to turn in. Suddenly, Livvie pulled open the cupboard and shouted, "Boo!"

Ruth squealed and tumbled out into Livvie's waiting arms. They both fell onto the soft floor and laughed at their own silliness. Ruth laughed until the tears streamed down her cheeks and her cough started again, until suddenly, she couldn't catch her breath. Panic spread through her as she gasped for air and pain gripped at her throat. Livvie's hands were on her face and Ruth was blinking back the tears, trying to focus.

"It's okay, Roo. Just breathe. You can copy me, watch."

Livvie started to take deep breaths in through her nose and out through her mouth. It was the same as how Ruth remembered the doctors showing her. She focused on Livvie's steady hands against her cheeks, which were a contrast to her own shaking ones. She looked into her friend's eyes and copied Livvie's actions. The panic began to ease, and her breathing got a little smoother. Her chest still hurt, and she needed to get back to her room and use the special mask her doctor gave her for when this happened. But right now, she was breathing, and she was safe. Livvie made Ruth feel safe.

❖

"Olivia Niamh Bell, what's this I hear about you kidnapping someone yesterday?"

Livvie looked sheepish as Dr Sutton walked into the room, clipboard in hand and eyebrow raised.

"In my defence, the playroom isn't big enough for hide and seek. Plus, I didn't kidnap, I brought her back. She looked sad and then she wasn't sad anymore. Isn't that a good thing?"

One of the younger doctors on Dr Sutton's team snickered and Livvie grinned.

"Maybe next time let someone know your plans, so if something bad happens, people know where to find you, hmm?" Dr Sutton said with a raised eyebrow.

"Mac saw us go, I made sure to wave. She knew where I was. Plus, there's not many places you can go that aren't locked around here anyways. I've tried." She mumbled that last part under her breath, but by Dr Sutton's head shake, she knew he heard it.

He focused his attention on Gracie and her mom, who had barely glanced in their direction for the short conversation. Livvie took that as her cue to duck out and go find Roo. She'd spent most of her day in school thinking about ways to make Roo laugh like she had yesterday. She didn't mind that Roo didn't talk to her, but seeing her laugh had made Livvie's belly squeeze happily, and she wanted to do that again. There weren't many new things to do in the hospital after the first few weeks, and there were only so many times she could watch the same movies they had on videotape or play a board game with whichever nurse wasn't too busy.

Most of the other kids here didn't stay long, and for the time they were there they rarely left their rooms. She waved through the windows and made funny faces at the ones who looked like they needed cheering up. Sometimes she played with someone in the playroom, but most of the time Livvie was alone. She was used to that, but now the thought of seeing Roo made her excited to come to the hospital. Roo didn't ask her questions about Gracie or talk about how lucky she was to get to hang out in a room full of toys every day rather than doing homework. Roo didn't pretend to understand or say she was sorry. She was happy to be with Livvie, listening to her, paying attention to her and nobody else. And Livvie wanted to hold on to that feeling for as long as possible.

She skipped toward the playroom and hummed along the way. The quiet buzz of machines she hardly registered anymore accompanied her tune. Roo wasn't in the playroom when she walked in, so she set about pulling out the brick house. It was her best yet, especially with Roo's help. It was their house now. Roo had beaten her to the playroom the past few days, but Livvie knew how things went in here. There were always doctors or nurses or interruptions. As she started putting more pieces onto the structure, a sinking feeling settled in her stomach. She kept glancing toward the door, but nobody came, and the fear bubbling up inside got louder.

It was her fault. She'd scared Roo yesterday when they

played hide and seek, and now they wouldn't let her come play anymore. Or maybe Roo was too sick after the coughing. Livvie couldn't wait any longer with all the bad thoughts swirling through her head about what might be wrong. She had to go find out, say sorry, make sure Roo was okay. Maybe they'd let her play in Roo's room for a little while. She got up and headed in the direction of the room she had seen Roo enter before. She hesitated a little with her hand on the handle. Livvie knew from previous experience that going into another patient's room without a grown-up could get her into a lot of trouble.

But the fear of getting into trouble had never been enough to stop her doing what she wanted, and today was no different. She pressed the handle down and walked into the room. Light from the windows showed her how empty it was. She frowned as she took in the scene before her. It wasn't empty because Greta had taken Roo for a walk, or because Roo had gone to get a test done. No, that kind of empty was just empty of people, but there would still be stuff. People came with stuff.

The hospital bed was clean and freshly made. The locker was bare and there were no bags or clothes or toys strewn around like in Gracie's room. She was about to walk back out and check in case she remembered the room wrong when a piece of paper caught her eye. It was on the table at the end of the bed. The only remaining item in the room that wasn't part of the regular furniture. As Livvie picked up the solitary sheet, her eyes prickled with unfamiliar tears. Livvie rarely cried. She was the tough one, the strong one, the easy one. The one who could take care of herself. That's what everyone said, and she wore it like a badge of honour.

She didn't cry the time her mom forgot to give her her birthday gifts until after dark because Gracie was having a bad week. Or the time she looked into the audience at her school play and saw the sea of faces smiling and waving at their kids, but no familiar face looked back at her. She didn't even cry the time Gracie got super sick at home and her mom was so upset and yelled at her to call for help. She knew what her mom needed and what Gracie needed. She stayed calm, picked up the phone, and called for an ambulance. No tears to be seen, even when her heart beat with fear.

She stared down at the colourful pencil drawing of two stick figures standing with a LEGO brick house between them. Her eyes jumped to the scrawled words *Livy and Roo* at the bottom of the page, and she couldn't hold back the hot drops that slid down her cheeks and splattered onto the page. As the door opened behind her, she swiped at her eyes and quickly folded the sheet. She tucked it into the pocket of her grey tracksuit bottoms. She turned as Mac, the nurse she knew best, walked into the room and placed a hand on her shoulder.

"What're you doing in here, sweetheart?"

Livvie shrugged. She didn't trust herself to speak with the lump lodged in her throat. She managed to choke out one quiet word, hoping Mac would fill in the blanks.

"Roo?"

Mac smiled at her sadly, the same sad smile she had seen in this hospital on far too many faces.

"I'm sorry you didn't get to say goodbye, hon. The doctor discharged her this morning, and her aunt wanted to hit the road pretty quickly. They had a long drive back to Greta's place and she wanted to get there before it got dark."

Livvie nodded Mac led her from the room and toward Gracie's. She couldn't face going back there, not yet. She sidestepped Mac and brushed off the concerned look as she mumbled about leaving something in the playroom. She walked back to the room as a heaviness settled over her. Why was she surprised? People left here all the time without saying goodbye. It had never mattered much before. It was a good thing, right? It meant Roo was better. She was okay. That's what everyone wanted in here, to get to go home. So why did it make Livvie's stomach fill with all this bubbling sadness?

She walked into the playroom and glared at the offending reminder in the middle of the room. The sadness gave way to a more familiar feeling: anger. A feeling she was used to keeping to herself and only letting it out in the quiet of her bedroom when nobody was around to witness. She picked up the brick house and threw it onto the floor, watching the pieces fall apart as she refused to let any more tears fall.

CHAPTER ONE

R uth stepped off the train at the platform and took in the familiar surroundings as a sense of calm engulfed her. She glanced at the sign she had seen more times than she could count hanging from an old-fashioned pole that was older than she was, tracing the letters with her eyes.

Welcome to Wicker Hill.

It had taken a while after she first moved there with her aunt for Wicker Hill to feel like anything other than a surreal setting for a very vivid nightmare. Ruth often marvelled at the fact that it had been twenty years since the day with the longest car journey of her life. Most of the details were fuzzy by now, but the feelings she could recall with glaring accuracy. Slowly, throughout those first years, without her even noticing, Wicker Hill had become home.

Ruth's phone buzzed from her pocket, and she pulled it out. She smiled at the name that lit up her screen. Those pesky butterflies that had been swarming her stomach far too often lately woke up.

Make it there safely?

She read the four simple words. They were nothing too monumental to get excited over, but the butterflies stayed all the same. Her fingers hovered over the buttons to reply.

I arrived at my destination without incident. Well, except for the fact that they weren't serving coffee on board. Trains are supposed to be one of the safest ways to travel, but how safe is a journey without coffee?

Although they hadn't met in person yet, Ollie had become a part of her days so quickly that it scared Ruth a little. Her sadly sparse love life had left her downhearted more than usual when she moved to the city. Photographing happy couples on their wedding day pushed her to take action to find her own romance, but going out to meet someone in real life had seemed all too terrifying. So Ruth had fled to the relative safety of an app and expected to maybe meet a few people and get herself out there.

It had been three weeks since the first message dropped in her inbox from Ollie, and they had yet to go a day without talking. Text messages were safe, and right now Ruth needed that sense of safety. Even if the photos she'd seen of Ollie made her want to forget about her fears and dive right in headfirst. Which was even more of a reason not to.

She gripped the straps of her backpack where they fell over her shoulder and walked out of the station. She chuckled to herself at even calling it a station. One platform, a ticket machine, and a rusty old pole did not a station make. She turned left and took the short walk toward the village. It was a journey she barely registered now she was so accustomed to it.

Spring was in full bloom, with an array of colourful fresh flowers filling the picture-perfect plant boxes dotting the sides of the small bridge leading into the main street. She stopped about halfway across the bridge and paused to take in the postcard view ahead. The journey might be a familiar one, but she never failed to marvel at the idyllic village that housed the majority of her memories.

Ruth took out her phone and captured a quick shot. It was

a mirror image of many already saved in her photo app, but she loved to compare them and notice the barely perceptible differences over the years. Some things never seemed to change, yet one day suddenly everything would be different. It was a fact she found easier to swallow when she took time to look for the smaller changes. It had become a game she played, one that made her attention to detail a core part of her photography.

Ruth sent the photo to Ollie and smiled. The thought of sharing this little part of her world with someone new filled her with something she couldn't quite put her finger on. Ollie's reply had landed before she even had a chance to put her phone back into her pocket.

Looks like those postcards the tourists pay a fortune for. No wonder the city was a disappointment when you grew up on a Disney set.

Ruth took in the quaint two-bedroom cottage ahead as she meandered down the small winding dirt path. Her first glimpse of the cottage had reminded her of *Hansel and Gretel*, and fear gripped her despite the fact that her aunt definitely didn't seem like a scary witch. Ollie's remarks were more accurate, though. It did look like something from a Disney movie. She took another photo, this time of the cottage, and sent it to Ollie with a caption.

Fairy-tale cottage and all.

Ruth pushed open the unlocked door as her barely used key sat in the backpack pocket. Nobody locked anything in Wicker Hill. It was one of the only places she knew that still enforced the honour system to great effect. Before she was even through the door she was knocked back by a surprisingly heavy force, a force that was currently trying its best to lick her face. She dropped her bag and sat on the floor to give her full attention to the slobbering dog panting in front of her.

"Hey, sweet girl. I missed you, too."

She would never tire of the enthusiastic greeting she received from the jet-black pug that had become her best friend since the day ten years ago that Greta brought the little pup home.

"Leave the girl get through the door first, Pig."

Ruth smiled at her aunt's words as Greta walked through the doorway from the hall and took in the scene with amusement. The small black furball had shown up at the shelter Greta volunteered in with a tag on the collar saying *Piglet.* When nobody came to claim her, Greta took her home. It was fate, Ruth swore to this day, Roo and Piglet were meant to be.

Ruth got up from the floor and walked to the small kitchen as Piglet followed by her legs before she wandered off to the far too big, cosy dog bed in the corner. She spent the majority of her time these days sleeping in her bed or resting across Ruth's feet.

As Ruth entered the kitchen, Greta wrapped her arms around Ruth in a short, tight hug. Ruth breathed in the scent of familiar perfume as a sense of calm engulfed her. No changes there.

"I have lunch ready on the table, and the kettle's boiled for tea. Do you want to throw your stuff in your room first?"

Ruth was grateful for the woman who had turned her whole life on its head for her. It was something that she thought of a lot when she lived alone in the city and pined for the comfort of Greta and their cottage. A comfort that wrapped around her the minute she walked through that door. Ruth was also grateful for the home-cooked meal she had been sorely missing. She shook herself as she took in Greta's quizzical look.

"You okay, sweetheart?"

"Yeah, just tired from the train. I'm good."

Greta gave her a look she had seen so many times it made her grin. The *I know that's not the full story, but I'll leave you come to me in your own time* sort of look. It was funny how many words a face could portray.

Ruth went back to grab her bag and headed down the short hall to her bedroom on the right. She dropped the bag at the end of her bed and sat for a moment as she traced her fingers over the quilt Greta had made her for her twenty-first birthday. Truly, Ruth wasn't quite sure what was going on with her lately. A sense of nostalgia had overcome her from the minute she stepped onto the train this morning, and it was one she couldn't shake.

There was a part of Ruth that worried coming home meant she had failed. She had tried her hand at living in the city to give her photography a shot in a wider setting, and she couldn't even say she came home because that hadn't worked out. It had. She had made some great contacts in the visual art world. She had been booked at a number of queer events, and more than a few weddings, after some of her pieces were featured in an exhibition at a large pride event. She had done what she wanted to do and gotten her name out there.

But she was lonely, and in the quiet of her own thoughts, her anxiety had become unmanageable. The grounding and breathing techniques she had learned through years of therapy only went so far when so much of her time was spent within her own head. The city was small, as were most cities in Ireland, but it was huge in comparison to Wicker Hill. Ruth was just another person among a sea of people going about their days.

She ended her nights alone in her tiny apartment above a pub. It was loud and bright and so vastly different to everything that made her feel safe. But she had to get out of her comfort zone, right? That's what your twenties were for, and she was past the halfway mark of those. But she missed her cottage, she missed her aunt, she missed her dog. She missed home, so she had packed her bags and returned to the comfort of the familiar.

Ruth glanced out the window and saw the river flowing slowly at the end of the small hill. Her eyes travelled to the apples blooming on the tree to the right and the flowers blossoming around its base. No changes yet, it was all still the same as her last visit a few weeks ago. So why did everything suddenly feel so different?

❖

Olivia's phone chimed where it lay face down on the table and she stopped herself from grabbing it immediately. She was reluctant to give in to the almost addictive sensation that overcame her when a message announced itself so soon after she had sent one to Ruth. What had begun as a casual conversation a few weeks ago quickly turned into something Olivia would never have expected.

"You gonna check that or just stare at it until you absorb the message by osmosis?"

Olivia glared at her best friend Dani, who sat grinning at her from across the table. They were at Blaze, which was the local, and only, queer bar in the city. It had become their usual Saturday afternoon routine when Olivia wasn't on shift to grab lunch and talk about their weeks. Sometimes their friends joined them, but with more and more of them coupling up or dealing with babies, it was rare they all managed to be together at the same time.

"You're funny," Olivia deadpanned.

"So, are you doing the whole long-distance thing now that your girl has moved back to the back of beyond?" Dani asked.

"It's not the back of beyond. It has a train station, so it can't be that remote. And long distance is only for actual couples. This is casual. We're just talking."

When Olivia came across Ruth's profile on the dating app, the candid shots of the brunette had drawn her in immediately. The crinkle in Ruth's nose as the camera captured her mid-laugh made Olivia's heart squeeze in a way she wasn't accustomed to. The second photo of Ruth with arms wrapped around one of the most beautiful dogs Olivia had ever seen was the kicker, and she sent a message on the spot. It had been a couple of days before a reply landed in her inbox, and Olivia had barely remembered she was awaiting one.

"Ah yes. Just talking. All day, every day, from what I can tell. That sounds *super* casual to me," Dani mocked, and Olivia furrowed her brow dramatically.

Olivia had dipped her toes back into the dating pool a few months after moving to the city. That was almost a year ago now, and she had had some fun over that time. However, none of her interactions had left her thinking about someone the way she found herself thinking about Ruth. Their messages had begun in the usual get-to-know-you way, but something was different with Ruth than with the others. The small talk gave way to some real conversations much sooner than Olivia expected, but it was a refreshing change.

"I'm just kidding, Ollie. But you clearly like this girl. I'm a little surprised you two didn't meet up before she left to make sure all this energy was worth it, you know?" Dani added.

"I know. But I told you, things came up. Right now, we are keeping it to texting, and you know what? It's kind of good. We've talked so much the past few weeks about things that would take months to get to with casual dates here and there. But it keeps a sort of distance, too, so I'm not losing myself in it."

When they had tried to arrange a casual first date, Olivia had to cancel last minute due to her shift running over. She had explained about being a nurse and her unpredictable schedules to Ruth already. Ruth had seemed fine with it, but her last serious girlfriend had claimed to understand, too. Until the time came where it affected Eva, and how much of herself Olivia could offer her, which never seemed like enough. That time came much sooner than Olivia would have liked with Ruth. Olivia hadn't even had the chance to prove she was worth the effort yet, but Ruth had surprised her with genuine understanding. She hadn't pulled back or made Olivia feel even the tiniest bit guilty for it.

"I get not wanting to lose yourself, trust me. But make sure you're not holding back too much, either. I don't want you to try so hard not to repeat your relationship with Eva that you lose out on something good. I know how that feels all too well," Dani said.

"It worked out pretty good for you in the end, though, eh?" Olivia wagged her eyebrows as she pointed at the engagement ring on Dani's finger.

"Don't change the subject," Dani said, but the smile on her face was adorable. Olivia was happy for her friend that she had finally found her happily-ever-after. It made Olivia want that for herself, even if the thought still terrified her.

"I know. Honestly, I do. Like when Ruth cancelled last week's date, my mind immediately jumped to it being some sort of payback for me cancelling because of work. I hate that I even considered it, but you know that wouldn't have been an anomaly with Eva. And that's something I never want to repeat. It was like I had been waiting for that other shoe to drop with Ruth, so when she cancelled, I was so close to just not responding at all."

Dani nodded toward the phone before replying, "Judging

by the way your face lit up when that thing just pinged, I'm assuming you thought better of ghosting her like an asshole?"

"Well, I figured that Ruth deserved the same show of faith she'd given me when I cancelled. And I'm glad I did. If anything, I've felt even closer to Ruth since that. There were no games or trying to decipher what she meant, she just explained and I understood and that was that."

Ruth had opened up to Olivia about the reason she was unable to make their date. She explained that her anxiety disorder could be as unpredictable for her as Olivia's schedules were for Olivia. They didn't meet up that evening for dinner as planned, but they messaged at length about Ruth's anxiety and her desire to move back home. Although Olivia's heart sank at the thought of Ruth moving farther away, she also enjoyed their back-and-forth conversation. Part of her worried that moving things face-to-face would change their dynamic, and right now, the dynamic worked.

"Open communication can do wonders for a relationship. It's a pity it's not more popular. Whatever the reason was, I'm glad you gave her a chance to explain. Eva aside, I trust your judgement. You should, too."

Olivia nodded. She was glad Dani didn't ask her why Ruth had cancelled. It was Ruth's story to tell, not hers, and she was just happy Ruth had trusted her with the information. When Olivia asked Ruth if there were ways she could help make any future meeting easier, the dots had appeared and disappeared for minutes before a reply came through from Ruth.

Nobody has ever asked me that before.

Olivia had been unhappy to hear that she was the first to offer Ruth what she viewed as bare minimum respect in the world of dating. She had carefully worded her response, not wanting to make assumptions about any past partners Ruth had, but unable to say nothing.

I'm sorry to be the first, but happy to set a new standard. We could make a list?

That last part had been sure to bring a smile to Ruth's face. Olivia had discovered her love of all things in list form from their earlier conversations. Sure enough, a minute later her phone had chimed again.

Now you're just flirting.

Ruth's reply had made Olivia smile at the time, and she smiled again just thinking about it.

"What's that smile? Wait, has she sent you naked pics that you're daydreaming about right now?"

"Seriously, Dani? Firstly, if she had, I wouldn't tell you. Secondly, I'm smiling about lists. Not everyone has their mind in the gutter."

"Lists?" Dani spoke the word in a way that clearly indicated her disbelief.

"She likes lists," Olivia replied without further explanation.

"Well, I'm glad you didn't let things with Eva derail this. Obviously, I want you to be careful with meeting strangers from the internet, but I love seeing you happy. And you've been happier the past few weeks than I've seen you since you got here. Even *lists* make you look all gooey eyed."

Olivia chuckled, but Dani was right. Ruth's messages had quickly become the best parts of her day. Ruth had started to send her random photos of things she was doing, which made Olivia feel involved in her day-to-day activities. Olivia had never anticipated mundane images so much in her life. They'd discuss regular life things along with deeper more meaningful thoughts, and of course flirted in between each and every topic.

"Somebody's eager." Dani laughed as Olivia's phone chimed again. She quickly picked it up this time. Olivia wasn't one to play hard to get, and she knew it was futile to pretend like she wasn't eager to reply. Dani knew her too well to fall for that. Olivia frowned at the message that appeared above the one she had been anticipating from Ruth. A tight feeling squeezed her stomach as she scanned the preview.

Ring asap. It's dad.

Her sister's message was as vague as always, but those last two words had Olivia wishing she'd left the phone face down for a little longer. She ignored the message for a moment to open Ruth's far more appealing text. Olivia took in the picturesque cottage in the photo before she looked out the rain-streaked window of the bar. It was still bright enough to see the litter-filled street outside. The cottage was certainly a far cry from the Ireland Olivia currently lived in. Nobody would want a postcard of this place.

"What's wrong?" Dani asked with a concerned tone.

"Grace texted. She asked me to call," Olivia replied.

"I know that face doesn't come from the prospect of talking to Gracie. What else?" Dani asked.

"She said it's about Henry."

Dani grimaced and her face looked about how Olivia felt. Dani was one of the few people in Olivia's life who knew much of her family dynamics. They had grown up together, so Dani knew Olivia as well as anybody did. Olivia was grateful that she didn't have to offer up any further explanation.

"I should call," Olivia said with reluctance.

"I'll grab us a couple more drinks."

Dani hopped up and gave Olivia some privacy as she pressed call on Grace's number and braced herself for whatever was about to come.

"Livvie, finally."

Olivia bristled at the childhood nickname that she rarely heard anymore. It was just Grace and her mom that used it now, since she went by Ollie or Olivia everywhere else in her life. The name reminded Olivia of days she would rather forget, and she had lost count of the number of times she had gently corrected Grace on its use before giving up.

"You texted me about three minutes ago. Dramatic much?"

There was a soft sniffle on the other end of the line and Olivia's heart sank.

"Gracie, what's wrong? What happened?"

Her sister definitely had a flair for the dramatic, but quiet sobbing wasn't part of her gig. Olivia had never been one to take her sister's pain, physical or emotional, lightly.

"He's really sick, Liv. I don't know what to do."

Olivia's grip tightened around the phone pressed against her ear, and her muscles tensed. Henry had been diagnosed with end stage liver failure a few years ago, and it had been a double-edged sword for Olivia. End stage seemed so final, but liver failure wasn't quite that straightforward. The self-inflicted nature of the disease for Henry left a myriad of emotions that Olivia was still sorting through, some she was sure she'd never fully come to terms with.

"What's his nurse saying? Are you there? Put me onto her."

Henry lived near a rural village a couple of hours' drive from the city. Despite the fact that he'd lived there since Olivia was a teenager, Olivia had never made the trip there. In fact, it had been a number of years now since she had seen him at all. Grace was a more frequent visitor and would update Olivia on anything relevant. Grace knew it was a sore subject for Olivia.

They had experienced their childhoods and being parented differently, not just by Henry, but by their mom, too. Although Olivia still had a relationship with her mom, it was strained and filled with a lot more baggage than Grace's. Their mom had always been careful to shield Grace from her vitriol when it came to Henry, but Olivia got no such protection. Olivia had always been her mother's confidant, even when she was far too young to understand her mother's feelings. Despite their different experiences with their parents, Grace was always careful not to pull Olivia in unless she needed to.

"He fired her. The nurse. He's saying he won't leave any stranger here to watch him die. He's not making sense some of the time, and I'm trying to take care of him, but Livvie…I'm scared."

Olivia's heart cracked on those last words as Grace's voice hitched. Olivia's mind was being pulled in far too many directions to think straight. Dani returned with their drinks and gave her a look filled with concern as Olivia gripped the edge of the table.

"When did he fire her?"

The pause on the other line was all Olivia needed to have her up out of the seat and wondering where her suitcase was in her apartment.

"A couple of weeks. I was trying to take care of it. I know you don't want to be—"

"Send me the address or Eircode for my maps. I need to call work and get some things together, but I'll be there tomorrow, Gracie."

Olivia heard the softly whispered thank you as she ended the call. *Two weeks.* Her little sister had been dealing with this alone for two whole weeks, because she wanted to protect Olivia from the pain that would undoubtedly come.

"Be where?" Dani asked with a frown.

"Grace has been trying to care for Henry alone and she's struggling. I need to go."

Olivia grabbed her jacket from the back of the chair and pulled up the taxi app on her phone.

"Hold up. Sit back down and talk to me. You're not going anywhere tonight, so just take a breath."

Olivia stood rigid for a moment as Dani stared her down. Eventually, she slid back into the seat and sighed.

"I know you're going to try to talk me out of it, but you didn't hear Grace on the phone. She needs me, Dani."

Olivia knew that when she got under her covers tonight, not knowing exactly when she'd be back to sleep in her own bed, she would be overwhelmed with emotion. But right now, all she could think of was Grace struggling and alone.

"I hear you. And I also know nothing in the world will keep you from being by your sister's side when she needs you. Taking care of other people is your forte. But I'm not letting you rush out of here without at least making a plan with me, so I know you're taking care of you, too. That's the part you're not so great at." Dani reached across the table and squeezed Olivia's hand.

"I'm not sure any plan is going to help with taking care of a parent who never took care of me. But what am I supposed to do? He fired his nurses. He said he won't have strangers there. I'm a nurse, and his daughter, so it's the logical conclusion that I should be the one to do it instead. Except Grace is forgetting one thing. I'm a stranger, too."

"Which is why I want to know you won't just dive headfirst into caretaker mode and forget about your own needs. You've been doing it for years with your mom. She calls and needs something, and you drop and go. No matter what you're dealing with yourself. That's hard enough with one parent, but with two?"

Olivia's hand shook beneath Dani's, and she focused on steadying it.

"This is for Grace, not him. Henry isn't part of the reasons behind this decision. I know that's something I'll have to work through at some point, but right now Gracie needs me."

That was something Olivia knew how to deal with. She'd been doing it her whole life.

CHAPTER TWO

R uth woke the next morning to the sensation of warm breath on her face, and her eyes shot open.

"Jesus, Pig. You scared me."

The pug stared for a moment before tilting her head innocently. Ruth couldn't be mad at that face for long, and she sometimes swore her dog knew it. She checked her phone first thing, a habit that had formed over the past number of weeks, and sighed at the lack of new notifications. *Was the cottage photo too much?* It wasn't like one night without a reply was unusual in the grand scheme of things, but it was outside the norm she and Ollie had developed. Especially since Ollie wasn't on shift the night before.

Ruth threw on grey sweatpants and her favourite hoodie before heading to grab Pig's leash. Her aunt had already gone to work, but there were freshly made pancakes on the table ready to be heated, and her heart warmed. The sky was cloudy, and she grabbed her raincoat, forgoing the umbrella since Piglet wouldn't walk for long these days anyway. She made her way down to the village in search of what she swore was the best coffee in the world.

"Well, if it isn't my favourite girl on this planet."

Ruth's best friend Sophie made a beeline for Piglet and

got slobbery kisses in return as Ruth stood beside her dog waiting to be greeted.

"Well, hello to you, too, Soph."

"Oh hey, Roo. Didn't notice you there." Sophie aimed a cheeky grin Ruth's way before pulling her in for a hug.

"You're home." Sophie spoke the words softly as she held Ruth in the hug a little longer than their normal. Although they'd talked on the phone at least a few times a week while Ruth lived in the city, it had been strange not seeing Sophie every day. After Ruth moved to Wicker Hill with her aunt, Sophie had been the first friend she made. They had been a staple in each other's lives ever since. Their relationship had ebbed and flowed in its intensity throughout the years, but Sophie was the closest thing Ruth had to a sibling.

"How could I stay away? No coffee can compare."

Sophie's family owned the one and only café the village had to offer, aptly named Wicker Hill Café, and Sophie had taken over running it a few years ago. The selection was limited but the quality never failed, and Ruth had yet to find anywhere that lived up to Sophie's signature coffee blend. It had become so popular that they put it online to order in limited batches and sold out every time.

"Oh, I get it, you only want me for my coffee," Sophie huffed. She set about making a takeaway cup at the window latch, which was a more recent addition for orders to go.

"Well, you only want me for my dog, so I think it's fair."

Ruth shrugged as Sophie popped a dog treat out the window to a waiting Piglet, who knew what was in store.

"Touché. It's quiet at the moment. If you have a minute to hang out, I can join you."

Ruth grabbed a seat at one of the two small outdoor tables beneath the window as Sophie brought the coffee out. Ruth inhaled the steam rising from the cup and sighed happily before taking the first glorious sip.

"This is the best thing I've ever had in my mouth."

Sophie quirked an eyebrow as Ruth replayed the words in her head.

"Not even taking that back," Ruth mumbled before she took another sip of the piping hot liquid.

"You need to get out more, then. Did you hook up with hot nurse lady yet? If so, that statement is far more disappointing."

Ruth laughed and shook her head. "No, well, we're still talking, we just haven't met up yet. I think we're still talking, anyway."

"You think? Isn't that something that would be pretty obvious?"

Ruth shrugged and took a moment to check her phone to confirm that it was still sans message.

"You'd think. I sent her a photo yesterday when I got back, and she hasn't replied yet."

Sophie winced. "No reply to a raunchy photo? That's harsh. Does she have read receipts turned on? Because that would totally be worse."

"What? No, no raunchy photos. It was just a photo of the cottage. And what are read receipts?" Ruth asked.

"Oh boy, do I have so much more to teach you, Ruthie. Give me your phone."

Ruth handed over her phone as Sophie put in her passcode, which of course she guessed on the first try, and checked the last message to Ollie.

"See, here. It says delivered but not read. So, she may not even have seen the message yet. It's only been a day. Not even a day at that, it's still early. I realize that's like a week in lesbian time, but don't lose hope yet."

Ruth grabbed her phone back and scowled at Sophie.

"Stop stereotyping. And I'm pansexual, so at the very least, stereotype accurately."

"Yeah, but she's a lesbian so it still counts. Plus, isn't that more of a sapphic stereotype than strictly a lesbian one?"

Ruth bit back her sarcastic response. Any verbal reply would be met with another retort, so she didn't bother offering one. They sat in silence for a few minutes as Piglet lay happily at Sophie's feet and Ruth savoured the coffee that would be gone far too soon.

"I really like her, Soph." The words were little more than a whisper, and they were spoken before Ruth even thought them through.

"I know you do, love. I could tell that by talking to you on the phone about it, before I even saw this sappy look come over your face when you talk about her."

Sophie pointed at Ruth's face as if to emphasize her words, and like she had conjured it herself, Ruth's phone beeped. She tried to play it cool but failed when Ollie's name lit up her screen, and she sighed in relief.

"I don't need two guesses to know who that is. Point wholly proven."

Ruth took a moment to stick out her tongue in the childish manner only Sophie provoked in her, before she focused her full attention back to her phone.

You really do live in a Disney movie. It looks like something you'd find in the Hundred Acre Wood.

Ruth chuckled and snapped a quick photo of Piglet.

Piglet and all.

She frowned after hitting send and began typing again.

That's my dog's name, Piglet. It's not like a weird looking baby pig.

"Is this what you call flirting? Ruthie, you need help."

Sophie had somehow manoeuvred herself to peer over Ruth's shoulder while she was engrossed in her messages that lacked context.

Adorable. The dog's pretty cute, too.

"Ohh, she's better at this than you," Sophie said.

"Hush." Ruth turned her phone screen and glared at Sophie until she slinked back to her seat. "Don't you have work to do or something?"

Sophie looked to her right and left before focusing her gaze back on Ruth.

"I don't see any lines forming. There's a couple hundred people in this village, and I can practically predict exactly when each and every one of them will drop by. We've got at least another forty minutes before Mr B.'s daughter comes to get her usual morning to-go order."

That brought Ruth's attention away from grinning at her phone to ask, "How is Mr B. doing? I haven't seen his daughter in a long time, so I'm guessing not well."

Mr B., as he was known to anyone in Wicker Hill below the age of thirty, was the local postman. Ruth remembered how grateful she had been for his move to the village, about five years after her own, because it meant she wasn't the newest resident anymore. New people were a novelty there, and Ruth wanted to be anything but the centre of attention.

"He's hanging in there, but I don't think they are very hopeful. It's sad. I've called round to drop off cakes and coffee a few times and he seems like his old self, but he got confused a couple of times about who I was. I could see how tired he was. His daughter has been back for a couple of weeks now."

Apart from being grateful for the attention he took away from her, Ruth had a lot of time for Mr B. He had taken to leaving a little chocolate with the mail some days, and it was a small gesture that had stuck with Ruth. Sometimes, when the grief or anxiety would weigh heavier than she could bear, those small gestures were a big part of bringing light into her day.

"I'll need to pop over and visit soon. If he'd be up to it. Maybe I'll try to grab his daughter here one day and check what she thinks."

The sky had gotten duller in the space of time she'd spent at the café, and the first drops of rain started to fall.

"I better go before it gets worse," Ruth said. She tugged at Piglet's leash to get the dog to move. Piglet looked at her and stood, albeit reluctantly.

"She's here at the same time every morning, so pop by again tomorrow. I'm sure he would love to see you."

Ruth nodded and said her goodbyes before she made her way back down the street. The rain picked up and had her running down the path toward her cottage. Her clothes were clinging to her skin by the time she got through the door. Piglet trotted off to roll around her bed and dry herself on the blankets that she would have to lie on. *Not a smart move, Pig.*

Before she could talk herself out of it, Ruth snapped another photo. This time it was of herself with rain-slicked hair clung around her face and obvious water droplets falling down her cheeks.

Does it rain in fairy tales? Feels like there should've been birds holding umbrellas above my head or something.

She walked into the bathroom and turned the shower on to let the water heat as she stripped off her wet clothes. She grabbed her phone to put on her shower playlist and, she allowed herself to admit, to check for a reply.

But then I wouldn't have gotten to see this photo, which would've been a travesty. You do realize you can also hold your own umbrella, though, right? You're a strong independent woman who don't need no birds.

Ruth laughed and took a minute to type a reply despite the shivers running through her body that willed her to enter the nice, hot shower.

Want, not need. I can be strong and independent and still want some fairy-tale moments. But alas, I'm hopping in the shower instead of frolicking with animated birds.

Ruth pressed play on the playlist and finally stood under the stream of hot water. She closed her eyes and allowed herself to picture Ollie's face. Her mention of a shower had been intentional, and she hoped it spurred the same thoughts in Ollie that it did for her.

❖

Olivia put the suitcase in the boot of her car and hopped in the front seat, reading the message again. Thoughts of exactly what fairy tale–worthy moments she and Ruth could conjure together in a shower flitted through her head. She closed her eyes and sighed, giving herself a moment to revel in the fantasy. She had been meaning to tell Ruth why she hadn't replied the night before, and the whirlwind her life had taken that she was about to embark on, but that hadn't happened.

The lightness Ruth's messages brought made her want to hold on to it a little longer, without the weight of her current situation overtaking it. She wasn't afraid to talk to Ruth about it, even if it was a bit early for the childhood traumas to come out to play. No, it wasn't fear that held her back. It was this feeling, the fantasy, pure and untouched by the realities of life.

I'm not going to pretend I'd pick animated birds over you in the shower.

Olivia typed the message and hesitated before backspacing. Too much. They'd flirted of course, and they'd broached more intimate conversations some nights, but right now in the light of day that felt a little too overt.

Add "create fairy-tale moments" to our list.

She plugged her phone in and switched to the maps app, popping in the Eircode her sister had sent. Time to head to the back ass of nowhere. Olivia wondered for a moment how they'd survived for so long without GPS, or Eircodes for that matter. If she were to simply go off the generic address of a rural house she'd never been to before, she would likely double her drive time. Not that that was a negative right about now.

The journey time was a little over two hours, which was plenty of time to occupy her thoughts with all the reasons she didn't want to be going. Her phone beeped again, and Olivia itched to check the readout, but she kept her focus on the road ahead. She could really do with the distraction Ruth brought right now.

About five minutes into her journey, Olivia pulled over to the side of the road. Her restless brain refused to go any farther. She could use the distraction, right? So why not ask for it?

I know you aren't great with last minute plans, so feel free to say no. But I have a long drive ahead of me and I could use a companion. I was thinking maybe we could do the phone call we've been meaning to have? I know it's last minute, so you probably have plans, but I had to give it a shot.

Olivia tapped send and her heart beat a little quicker. She didn't want Ruth to feel pressured to answer if she called unannounced, and she was fully aware that it was midday on a weekday. Ruth likely had things to do.

As Olivia pulled the car back onto the road and headed in the direction of Henry's house again, her phone started to ring.

Her beating heart picked up the pace even more as she swiped to answer the call.

"You called."

Way to state the obvious, Ollie. She chastised herself as Ruth's unfamiliar voice piped over the line.

"You asked me to. You meant now, right? Sorry, I didn't clarify. I just pressed call before I thought about it."

The hesitant rambling made Olivia smile, and she sat back to relax into her seat. Unfamiliar, but so very Ruth.

"Yep, I meant now. I'm already on the road."

There was a soft sigh from Ruth's end at Olivia's confirmation.

"Headed anywhere fun?"

Olivia should've anticipated this. Of course Ruth would ask where she was going. She didn't plan to lie to her, but she wasn't sure how much of the truth she was ready to divulge.

"Definitely not. I'm headed to the middle of nowhere according to my maps."

Ruth chuckled. "Don't sound so grouchy. The middle of nowhere isn't so bad. Fairy tales happen there, remember?"

"I remember. Not sure this trip will be filled with those fairy-tale moments, but a girl can dream. I'm going to my… father's place."

The moniker felt foreign leaving Olivia's lips. She hadn't called him anything but Henry in as long as she could remember, but that would require even further explanation. Olivia was already opening the conversation to go to places she wasn't sure she wanted to go, but the alternative was going there alone in her head. As she listened to Ruth's voice, Olivia knew that going there alone wasn't the best option on the table.

"I'm guessing by your voice it's not for a friendly visit. You don't have to talk about it, but I'm here if you want to."

Olivia had known that, but hearing it still helped. Ruth was there, and she wanted to listen. She had picked up the phone and called her, and Olivia knew how much Ruth hated phone calls. If that wasn't enough of an indicator, then nothing was.

"I haven't seen him in a while."

Olivia spoke the words softly, like dipping her toes into the pool to see if she was ready to commit to submerging.

"What's a while?"

The question made Olivia pause for a moment. How long *had* it been?

"I saw him briefly at my sister's eighteenth birthday party. She's turning twenty-two in a few months."

"Wow. So, it has been a while. How do you feel about visiting?"

Ruth's tone of voice was gentle and curious without making Olivia feel pressured.

"A lot of things, none of them very good. He wasn't around much when I was growing up. He's an alcoholic. He's sober now, and has been since I was a teenager, but by the time he got his act together too much had come between us. My sister is a lot younger, so she has a different relationship with him. He has always been there for her, at least, as far as she remembers."

Olivia wasn't a crier and never had been. She learned early that crying didn't get you anywhere. There was rarely anyone around to hear it. She swallowed the lump that appeared in her throat and hoped Ruth didn't notice the catch at the end of her words.

"I'm sorry. That must be tough. Especially seeing your sister experience a different father with the same person."

Ruth encapsulated in one sentence what most people

never understood. Yes, it had been Olivia's choice not to have a relationship with Henry when he got his life together. That never meant it hurt any less that Grace got the dad Olivia had always wanted. The parents she had always wanted, if she were honest with herself. A protective mother, an attentive father. Something Olivia could only dream about.

"It is. But I love her enough to not resent her for it. She deserves good parents."

"So did you."

The words were whispered so softly Olivia wasn't sure if she imagined them until Ruth spoke again.

"Sorry, I'm overstepping. You didn't ask for my opinion."

"No, it's okay. You're right, I did. But she's been through a lot, too, and I'm protective, always have been," Olivia replied.

"She's lucky, having a big sister to look out for her. I've always wondered what it would be like to have siblings."

Olivia smiled as she thought about Grace and the ways their relationship had formed throughout the years.

"It's not all sunshine and roses. We used to kill each other. But she's my sister, nobody else could be mean to her. That was my job."

Ruth laughed and they settled into a comfortable silence for a few minutes as Olivia looked ahead on the maps app to make sure she didn't miss the turn-off.

"So, you have no siblings, and you live in a cottage in the woods with Piglet. Is there an evil stepmother I should know about? Any dragons I need to fight?" Olivia asked.

"I can't even keep track of what story you think I'm living in. But no, no evil stepmothers to worry about. Just me, my aunt, and Piglet. Who will lick your face a lot but doesn't breathe fire, I promise."

Ruth had mentioned living with her aunt before but had never delved into why. Olivia wondered if now was the time to ask, considering she had spilled some of her own not so secret issues.

"I hope you mean the dog, and not your aunt."

Ruth laughed, and the sweet sound sent flutters around Olivia's stomach.

"If there's face licking by adorable dogs involved, I'm in," Olivia said.

Olivia was shocked when she looked at the map and realized how much time had passed already. Having Ruth there made the journey easier, and surprisingly enjoyable. Something Olivia wouldn't have believed possible when she first got into the car. They spoke about random things for a while, light-hearted conversation that made Olivia forget what was ahead of her. The roads got smaller and smaller the closer she got, and Ruth sat in silence with her as Olivia paid close attention to the map.

"You don't need to stay for the whole trip. I'm sure you have better things to be doing. But I'm really happy you called, the time has flown," Olivia said after she rounded a tight corner.

"I have you on speaker while I get dinner prepared, and I'm home alone, so unless you have an objection I'd like to stay with you until you get there," Ruth said.

"Thank you."

The words couldn't convey the way Ruth's sentence had made Olivia feel. Olivia was used to being the person who was there for others. Her sister, her mother, her patients. She wasn't used to someone being there for her in this way.

"So, what are you making for dinner?" Olivia asked.

"Toasted cheese sandwiches with Taytos," Ruth stated

matter-of-factly. As if that was supposed to make any sense at all.

"You're making toasties with Taytos and calling it dinner?" Olivia scoffed.

"It's food. Don't knock it. My culinary skills may be limited, but I have other skills that make up for it."

Olivia's mouth dropped open as a shiver rippled its way through her body at the implications.

"I didn't…that came out…ugh. Thank God this isn't a video call, or you'd see how red my face can go."

Olivia smiled as Ruth stuttered on the other end of the line.

"I'd definitely like to see that sometime."

Olivia lowered her voice as she spoke and decided to go all in while the moment was there. "Maybe when you're showcasing those other skills."

Ruth's breath hitched and Olivia smiled. She hoped she wasn't the only one feeling the heat of the moment.

"Only when you pay up on those fairy-tale moments you've promised me."

Ruth's voice didn't waver, and Olivia was surprised at the teasing tone.

"I never break a promise, darling."

The term of endearment slipped off Olivia's tongue in far too natural a way. If talking on the phone with Ruth brought this much out in Olivia, she was almost worried about what meeting in person could do.

"Somehow, I believe that," Ruth said.

"You sound surprised. Is it unusual for you to believe what someone says?" Olivia kept a hint of teasing in her voice to lighten her words, but she wanted to know the answer.

"It's more unusual for people to mean what they say."

Olivia wasn't quite sure how to reply to that, but before she could figure it out Ruth spoke again.

"I'm not as cynical as that sounded. I've just spent a lot of time trying to read between the lines of the words people use and figure out the real meaning. I just…I don't feel like I need to do that with you."

Olivia's heart squeezed at the idea that Ruth was comfortable saying this to her.

"You don't. If I ever say something you're unsure about, just ask me to clarify and I can do that. No games, no puzzles, okay? Well, none we don't both want to play at least."

Ruth chuckled softly and Olivia glanced at the map before letting out a sigh.

"I'm almost there, I think. It's a lot of small windy roads. I don't think the map is bringing me through a village because I've passed nothing but fields. It says the house is just up ahead. I'm really nervous."

That last part slipped out before Olivia could stop it.

"That's understandable. Take a deep breath and ground yourself before you go inside. And remember I'm right on the other end of the phone," Ruth replied.

"That makes me feel better. So do the photos. I love when you send them."

Olivia's mouth was apparently running away with itself as she pulled the car in beside her sister's familiar one, and her nerves kicked into high gear.

"Then I'll send plenty today and you can look at them later. I'm not getting up to much, so it'll mainly be of Piglet and me. You'll have to make do," Ruth said.

"How do you do that?" Olivia said softly.

"Do what?" Ruth asked.

"I'm parked now and so nervous, but now all I'm thinking about is how I can't wait for it to be later, so I can look at those photos. How do you make my day suddenly seem that much brighter?"

Olivia noticed the oak front door to the two-story detached house open as Grace peered out at her.

"It's a fairy tale, Ollie. That's how."

CHAPTER THREE

"S he came by this morning all high and mighty, you'd swear she had nothing to be ashamed of, not showing her face all this time."

Ruth was eavesdropping while she drank her coffee and waited for Sophie to finish serving Mrs Guiney, the village gossip. Or one of the many, at least. Living in a village as small as Wicker Hill, you soon learned that nothing stayed private for long, and your life was generally up for public opinion. It was rarely done with malicious intent. People were bored and nosy, which led to a dangerous combination.

"What was all that about?" Ruth asked as Sophie slid into the seat across from her.

"Oh, apparently Mr B.'s daughter is in town and showed up at the clinic this morning, demanding to talk to Dr Hegarty about his prescriptions and treatment plan and everything. Mrs Guiney was in for a check-up, so of course she has an opinion on it all."

"But what did she mean, showing her face? Didn't you say his daughter has been here for weeks? That's why I came by this morning, to check about visiting Mr B. You said she'd be by soon."

"Nice to know you weren't just coming to see my lovely face."

Ruth laughed at Sophie's dramatic pout.

"Yeah, no, not Grace. His other daughter. The older one who nobody has ever seen because she's never bothered to come visit. Remember he used to tell us stories about her before, what was her name again? Libby?"

Ruth shrugged. She had a fuzzy recollection of Mr B. talking about his daughter and how smart she was. He used to brag about her so much that it always made Ruth wonder if her own father would've done the same for her. Telling random people about her accomplishments, and people Ruth never met would go about knowing tidbits of her life. It was sweet to consider.

"Anyway, whatever her name is has come to town now. Better late than never, I suppose."

Ruth didn't know enough to comment, but she had wondered throughout the years why the mystery daughter never visited. It became more and more apparent, as Mr B. got sicker and travelled less, that they didn't have the close bond she always assumed they did from his bragging. Grace was the only visitor from outside of Wicker Hill that Ruth had ever known to stop by.

"I think she's a doctor or something because she seemed to know what she was talking about at the clinic. Oh, don't look now, but I think that's her. Maybe you can use the excuse of asking about visiting to get the low down on her. One thing I will say, she knows how to rock a suit."

Ruth was beyond curious to see what kind of woman wore a suit to the local village café, but didn't turn around right away. She was sure the rest of the patrons were already gawking, and having been at the other end of those stares all those years ago, she knew too well how intimidating it could be. Ruth slowly sipped her coffee and bided her time before looking back without making it too obvious.

"What can I get for you?" Sophie had gone to the counter to serve the other woman, and Ruth tilted her head to the side to catch a glance.

"My sister Grace said there should be an order ready for me to pick up. Can I add a plain black coffee to that, please?"

Ruth's pulse quickened at the silky-smooth voice that wrapped itself around her. She swivelled in her chair and almost knocked over the mug she had set on the table. Ruth needed to see the woman standing at the counter. Her face was turned to Sophie, but Ruth took in the long legs attached to the picture-perfect hourglass figure. She moved her eyes all the way up to the shoulder length chestnut brown hair framing the familiar face. The green eyes that Ruth recognized glanced her way, and they both froze.

"Is that everything? Are you okay?"

Ruth vaguely noticed Sophie glancing between them in her periphery, but she couldn't drag her eyes away. *How? Why?*

"Ollie?"

Ruth was surprised to find that she spoke first as the word fell from her lips while she sat in shock.

"Ollie? *Oh.* Ollie!" Sophie exclaimed. Her voice changed from confusion to excitement and snapped Ollie out of whatever daze she was in.

"Ruth. Wow. I wasn't expecting this."

Ruth's heart pounded so loudly as she sat rooted to her spot. She should move or say something, but it was all so bizarre. Ollie was there, in her village, in her best friend's café. Ollie, whom she had been flirting with an hour ago. Ollie, whom she spent hours talking to on the phone for the first time yesterday. She was there, standing in front of Ruth, and all Ruth could do was stare.

"This is awkward, isn't it?"

Ollie had her takeaway bag and cup in hand and had somehow made her way over toward Ruth, as Ruth finally got her legs moving enough to stand.

"It's…I don't even know what word fits. Why are you here? You're here."

Ollie laughed and the sound was familiar and foreign all at once.

"I'm here. I guess I should've paid more attention when I walked in this morning, and I probably would've recognized it from the photos. So, this is your fairy-tale village?"

None of this made any sense at all, and Ruth was struggling to catch up to everyone around her. That's when it clicked. The mystery daughter who never visited.

"You're Mr B.'s daughter."

Ollie's face darkened for a moment, and Ruth remembered their conversation yesterday.

"Sorry, I just mean…that's why you're here. When you said you were visiting your father, I didn't realize…"

"Yeah, sorry, I guess I'm just not used to being called that. I can't believe I never actually knew the name of your village. I wish I had asked now. I would've liked our first time meeting to be a little less of a surprise, given how much you hate them," Ollie said.

Ruth smiled. "I was actually waiting for you. I mean, not you, but your sister. I was going to ask about visiting, but…"

Ruth trailed off, unsure of how to continue. Ollie looked equally uncertain as she took a sip of the coffee in her hand.

"Holy shit, this is amazing. You never informed me you lived close to the best coffee ever invented," Ollie said.

Ruth laughed as the pounding of her heart finally slowed down.

"Yeah, it is amazing. One of my favourite parts of Wicker Hill," Ruth said.

Ollie looked at her for a moment, and Ruth felt a warmth creeping up her neck.

"I really need to get back with these, but...maybe you could show me your other favourite parts soon?" Ollie asked.

She nodded as Ollie turned and headed back up the road. Ruth stood and stared. All she could think was how the beautiful photos she had seen were nothing compared to Ollie, live and in person.

❖

What the hell just happened?

Olivia walked through the door to Henry's house and set the bag on the table as the scene looped through her mind on repeat. Right when she thought things couldn't get any more complex, life threw another curveball.

"You okay, Livvie?"

Grace bounded into the kitchen and grabbed food from the bag Olivia had placed on the table. She put the scones on to heat and set out the butter and jam. Olivia had no idea how to explain what had her so rattled, until she had time to process it herself, so she deflected.

"I popped by the clinic. I spoke to the receptionist, who said the doctor will give me a call later this afternoon to get me up to speed. She wouldn't give me much more than that until she confirmed with Henry, which is probably a good thing, since I'm virtually a stranger."

"It's weird when you call him Henry. And you're not a stranger, you're his daughter. Plus, as the oldest, you're technically next of kin, right?" Grace asked.

His daughter. That was the second time today she'd been called that. And although it was factual, it lodged a weird feeling in her gut.

"I assumed he put you down. But I'm a relative, so they'll talk to me once he confirms. I think the receptionist said the doctor would be by later today anyway, so I can catch up with him then. And find out why every nurse has been incompetent enough to be scared away by a frail old man."

"Be careful who you're calling old, Livvie. The frail part I'll give you." Henry walked into the kitchen. He pushed the walker in front of him as Grace rushed to his side to pull out a chair at the table.

"I'm fine, Gracie," Henry insisted. He leaned against the walker for support as he sat. But he wasn't fine, which was clear for anyone to see. Henry might not be old in years, but he had aged rapidly since the last time Olivia had seen him. The shock of that still hadn't worn off from yesterday when she first arrived.

Olivia busied herself going through the paperwork that Grace had set aside for her as Henry and Grace ate at the table.

"Why don't you join us, Livvie?" Henry asked.

The softly spoken words were hard to ignore, much as Olivia wished she could. She found that it was much easier as a teenager fuelled with anger to ignore the pleas of the tall, strong man who had abandoned her. Faced with a shell of the man she remembered and anger that had turned to hurt, it was harder to hold up the walls she'd surrounded herself with.

"I've got a few calls to make about the insurance, and I need to check in with work. But thanks."

Olivia added that last bit as she saw his shoulders droop even more before she turned and walked from the room. She walked up the stairs and pulled out her phone, smiling as she noticed a message from Ruth waiting for her. Her heart skipped a beat knowing that the potential of seeing her soon was far higher than she would've guessed earlier that morning. Olivia walked into the guest room that her sister had shown her to last night and plopped onto the bed.

I didn't picture you as a power suit kind of woman. It suits you, though.

Olivia smiled and turned onto her side as she lost herself for a moment in the thought of Ruth's gorgeous blue eyes staring into hers.

I'm usually a scrubs kind of woman, but I make an exception on occasion. I had to deal with some things for Henry, and dressing up gets people to listen better.

She had learned on more than one occasion that her usual jeans and T-shirts got her overlooked and underestimated. The bubble with three dots appeared and disappeared, then appeared again. Olivia felt like a giddy teenager, but she couldn't look away.

We don't get many people in suits around here, so it definitely turned heads. Mine included.

The fact that Ruth could make her squirm with simple words on a screen had her wondering what effect the teasing tone would have in person. Just as the thought weaved its way around her mind, a photo came through. It was an image of what she presumed were Ruth's feet dipped into a stream surrounded by wildflowers. The colour contrasts were beautiful. Ruth followed it up with another message.

This is one of my other favourite places. This stream has heard my deepest, darkest secrets. I'm sure you have a lot on right now with your dad, but I'd love to show it to you sometime.

Olivia stared at the photo again and imagined sitting beside Ruth and dipping her toes into the flowing stream. She pictured them lying back, fingers entwined, talking about all of those secrets as she unravelled each layer that made Ruth uniquely her.

I'd love that.

Olivia reluctantly set her phone aside and picked up the stack of documents that needed her attention. Considering Henry had been living with a failing liver for over a decade, she hoped he was prepared. But Olivia wasn't one to trust that people had done as they should, especially people who had let her down before. She planned to take the time, before her sister went back to college the following day, to see what needed to be done in what was likely the last few weeks of Henry's life.

Olivia wondered for a moment how Ruth would feel about her now, knowing she was treating preparing for her father's death like marking off a to do list. Especially since Ruth seemed to know Henry, or at least the person he had become since moving here. In fact, Ruth probably knew him better than Olivia did. Everyone in this small village would know the father Grace had. The man who showed up to his youngest daughter's birthday parties, who never missed a planned visit, who remembered important events and milestones.

None of them knew the man Olivia had grown up with. The one who disappeared for weeks on end. The one who broke promise after promise. The one who abandoned them while her baby sister was in hospital for so long it felt like a second home to them. The one who took the warm, caring mother Olivia barely remembered and left her with a sad, bitter version who had never fully recovered from the years of worry and pain.

Not only had Olivia grown up without a father to rely on, she had also been robbed of a mother to lean on for comfort or support. Henry might have been the one who left, but he hadn't been the only parent to abandon Olivia in her time of need. Her mom had become so consumed with her own pain and anger that anything she had left was given to Grace. Olivia took on the role of caretaker, for both Grace and her mom, and lost the remnants of her childhood in return.

Another photo came through and Olivia opened the message with an image of an old fashioned black wrought iron sign, emblazoned with the same words that Ruth typed in the caption.

Welcome to Wicker Hill.

CHAPTER FOUR

"Y ou failed to mention the fact that your online beau was hot AF."

Ruth threw a cushion across the couch at Sophie.

"Don't use text speak in real life, Soph. You can say the actual words without abbreviating. And I did in fact mention it," Ruth replied.

"No, you said she looked good in her photos. Understatement of the year, my love. That suit. *Phew.*" Sophie fanned herself to emphasize her words, and Ruth shook her head. Not that she disagreed. Ollie in that suit was an image that hadn't left her brain for long since they'd run into each other at the start of the week.

"So now that she's here and in town for the foreseeable, when are you getting it on?"

She couldn't blame Sophie for asking, even in her own crude way. It was a question Ruth herself had been considering. Proximity was no longer an issue, and after seeing Ollie in the flesh it was taking over most of Ruth's waking moments. A lot of her sleeping ones, too.

"Ollie's going through a lot right now dealing with her dad. Her sister went back to college Tuesday, so she's been doing it solo, and I guess there's a lot there to deal with since they aren't close enough for her to know everything."

"I don't get that. Mr B. is such a nice guy. I don't understand why she's not made an effort before now. Too little, too late, isn't it?"

Ruth bit back the urge to defend Ollie with facts because the little she did know wasn't her information to share.

"Families are complicated. We both know that. Not everything is as it seems, and she doesn't deserve judgement. Which is something our village can be far too good at doling out. Just don't fan the flames of the gossip mill on this, okay?"

Working in the only café in the village left Sophie in the prime position for hearing basically everything that happened. She had an unusual amount of power to steer gossip one way or another if she wanted to. It was a power Sophie generally used wisely, but Ruth knew it wouldn't hurt to ask.

"I hear you. I'll be good. It's a Friday night, though, why don't you text her and I can get out of your hair? Her sister will be home from college for the weekend, right? I know I joke, but it's been forever since I've seen you light up this way about anyone. I mean that literally. I've never seen you like this, and you haven't even kissed the woman. So, hop to it!"

Sophie made it sound so easy. Ruth was trying to balance her anxiety around bothering Ollie while she had so much on her plate, with her eagerness to be a friendly face for her right now in what she could only imagine was a lot of uncertainty.

"Where are we hopping to?" Greta asked as she walked in from work at the tail end of Sophie's sentence. Greta dropped her bag on the counter as Ruth shot a look toward Sophie. She hoped it was enough to indicate this wasn't a topic she wanted to delve into with her aunt yet. However, it was a look Sophie pretended not to notice.

"Ruth's hopping into bed with her used-to-be online and now here-in-person, real-life girlfriend," Sophie said.

"Soph!"

Ruth's aim with the cushion was far more precise this time and hit Sophie square in her big mouth.

"I feel very behind here. You have a girlfriend?" Greta raised an eyebrow and tilted her head at Ruth in the inquisitive yet reprimanding way only a parent could master.

"Not exactly," Ruth mumbled as she averted her eyes.

It wasn't that she was opposed to her aunt knowing about her love life. Greta was gay, so the girlfriend part wasn't a concern and never had been. Greta had always been very open about her sexuality, which in turn allowed Ruth to explore her own without fear. But her aunt had a tendency to be overprotective and wrap Ruth in cotton wool. Greta would have concerns about Ruth meeting people online, even though there were few other ways to meet people these days.

If Ruth were honest with herself, though, the truth was Ollie had been something that was hers and hers alone, up until now. A little slice of life outside of Wicker Hill. Though she adored her aunt and the beautiful village she grew up in, sometimes everyone knowing everything about you was overwhelming.

"So anyway, then Ollie shows up at the café in a made-for-TV movie moment, and they stare gooey eyed across the room at each other, and wouldn't ya know it, she's the long-lost daughter and—"

"Seriously, Sophie!" Ruth interjected after she snapped out of her thoughts enough to realize Sophie was mid-retelling of the whole story to Greta. Greta had joined them in the living room and seemed enthralled by the tale.

"You're making it sound much more dramatic than it was," Ruth said.

"I'm really not. I swear people started moving in slow motion around you both," Sophie replied.

Ruth couldn't help the laugh that sputtered out at that.

"Wait, you're talking about Olivia Bell. I met her Monday at the clinic. She seemed nice."

Greta was the receptionist at the one and only doctors' surgery in the village. *Olivia*. Ruth hadn't ever considered what Ollie was short for, but it made sense.

"So, do I need to make myself scarce then if you're inviting her over? I assume you can't go to hers, considering everything with her father," Greta asked.

Ruth's mouth fell open at the blasé way her aunt spoke. It was as if she wasn't talking about vacating the house so Ruth could get it on with someone she'd only ever laid eyes on once.

"I haven't even texted her yet. She's probably busy."

Ruth didn't want to get her hopes up. Sophie picked up Ruth's phone from the coffee table and pushed it in her face.

"So do it, before I do," Sophie threatened.

Ruth's eyes went wide. She didn't want to deal with the fallout of whatever message Sophie deemed appropriate. Ruth didn't want to jump Ollie's bones, which was probably where Sophie would start the conversation. Well, she did *want* that, but she wasn't ready for it. She did however want to spend more time with Ollie, however that looked.

Hey. I know things have been busy for you, but I wanted to check if you wanted to do something this eve? There's not much in the way of entertainment around here, but we could drive about twenty minutes away to the nearest restaurant, or you could come over here. No pressure.

Ruth chewed on her lip as she sent the message off and sensed two sets of eyes trained her way.

"She's likely not glued to her phone. Stop staring, you're making me nervous," Ruth said.

Her screen lit up with the silent indication of a reply as

Sophie and Greta pretended to busy themselves with other conversation topics.

That sounds like heaven. But as much as I'd love to see if the inside of the fairy-tale cottage looks as magical, I can't, I'm afraid. Grace isn't back until the morning. Henry isn't doing well, so I don't want to stray too far. I know he'll likely sleep the whole time, but I need to be on hand just in case.

Ruth deflated but tried to remind herself that this wasn't a rejection. Everything Ollie had said was perfectly understandable. Another message popped in before she had a chance to reply.

I would invite you around here, but the week hasn't been great, and I haven't even had time to shower or tidy. I've been living on leftovers and haven't even managed to get the basics of a meal in. Seeing you would've definitely made a terrible week a little better, though. Your photos have been the highlight of my days.

That last part perked her up a bit, and her disappointment turned to sadness for Ollie. Ruth wished she could do something, anything, to help. Suddenly, an idea popped into her head. As soon as the thought occurred, it took root, and she turned to Sophie.

"I need your help."

❖

Olivia had been a nurse for long enough to know the ups and downs of someone at the end of an illness. Although Henry's aged appearance had startled her when she arrived, he had been walking around aided by a walker, talking, and generally seemed in good spirits. Olivia wasn't sure if it was an act put on for her sake, or simply a couple of good days, but either way, it had been short lived. Since the day after Grace went back to college, Henry had been sleeping more than not, and his waking moments were clearly painful and difficult.

Olivia was almost grateful for the haze of confusion that made him think more often than not that she was any other nurse. The man lying in the bed was so far removed from the father she remembered that it also allowed her to think of him as any other patient. She spent the past few days bathing him, giving him food, making sure he took his medication, and everything else that generally came along with the job.

There were some moments however that were a stark reminder that this wasn't simply a job. As she went to check on Henry before finally grabbing a well-needed shower, he woke. His pain was evident in the moans that escaped his lips. He grabbed her wrist and stared at her with wide, glassy eyes.

"Livvie? My Livvie, is that you?"

The hint of hope in his voice added another chip to the wall Olivia was trying so hard to keep standing.

"Yeah, it's me. Let me grab your painkillers," Olivia replied.

She placed her hand above his on her wrist and tried to untangle herself from his grip. She needed to go back into nurse mode and attend to his needs. Henry placed his second hand on top of hers and held it firm.

"Livvie, you came. You're finally here," Henry said.

Slow tears started to fall down his cheeks, and Olivia was rooted to the spot as she stared into the green eyes that were so like her own.

"I'm so sorry, Livvie. I'll make it up to you, I promise. I'll take you to the arcade and we can play those games you love. They have a new ice cream machine. You'll love it. I'm better now."

Olivia swallowed the lump in her throat as she realized

Henry wasn't actually seeing her. He was seeing the pre-teen version of her that refused to visit him after he missed yet another one of her birthdays. His letters had mimicked the words he said now, filled with promises of arcades and sweets and as much ice cream as she could eat to make up for it. Promises she never gave him the chance to break again.

"Just rest now. It's okay," Olivia said.

It wasn't okay, but now wasn't the time to expect heartfelt apologies. Henry was sick, and her job at that moment was to take care of him. Olivia had no expectations or intentions of it becoming a tearful reunion. She was a nurse, and he was a patient, and they needed boundaries. Right now, she was the only one capable of maintaining them.

Olivia turned to walk out and get stronger painkillers so Henry could have a comfortable sleep. The crack in his voice stopped her briefly in her tracks.

"I love you, my little Livvie."

Olivia's legs seemed to move of their own accord, carrying her to fulfil the task on autopilot as her mind got lost in a sea of memories. She remembered the times those words filled her with such comfort and happiness. It was something she hadn't allowed herself to recall since that same birthday all those years ago. They were placed in a box in her head and locked up tight. Olivia needed to make sure they went back where they belonged so she could survive the next few weeks and go back to the life she had created for herself.

After she got Henry settled again and made sure he was sleeping soundly, Olivia stepped beneath the stream of hot water to wash off the long week. Her muscles ached almost as much as her heart, but she focused on the former and allowed the spray of water to hit every knot that had formed. She thought about the messages Ruth had sent earlier, and a wave of longing overcame her. Part of her wanted to say screw it all and ask Ruth to come over and help her forget the hell she'd been thrust into. The only bright spot in this week had been Ruth. Knowing Ruth was so close made Olivia long to get lost in the chemistry they clearly shared.

But one look around the house was enough to dissuade her from that decision. Any spare moment Olivia had while Henry slept had been spent poring over documents, figuring out what bills needed paying, or answering the phone to one of the many people who kept ringing to check in on Henry. The first time she answered the landline she assumed it would be a scam call. *Who even has landlines these days?* But no, it turned out Henry had a lot of people in his life, many of whom checked up on him daily.

That left little time for tidying, a skill Olivia had never quite mastered in the first place. It was much easier to keep her small one-bedroom apartment in the city clean when she rarely ate there and didn't own much stuff. It was more difficult in a large, unfamiliar house that she hadn't left in days. Takeout containers piled up, alongside piles of papers, and mugs of tea and coffee. Olivia was craving coffee, or more accurately the liquid heaven from that small place where she had bumped into Ruth. But even though it was a relatively short walk to the town, Olivia had been too concerned to leave Henry unattended to make the trip.

Grace would be back tomorrow, and Olivia could show her face in the village then. But tonight, she planned to hole up with the remaining food from last night's takeaway and binge *Wynonna Earp* on her laptop in the guest room. There was nothing quite as comforting as watching strong women kick some demon ass.

Once she could give Henry his final dose of medication, she would go to sleep herself. The doorbell rang and Olivia checked the clock. She wondered who would wait until this time of the evening to visit. Olivia would tell them Henry was sleeping and send them on their way so she could wallow alone in peace.

Olivia opened the door to nobody and spotted two overflowing bags on the porch. Grace had mentioned some of Henry's friends from the village occasionally dropped home-cooked meals off when they visited, but why wouldn't they wait around to say hello? She grabbed the bags and headed inside as she noticed a note pinned to the top of one.

Dinner is in the blue bag. There's a couple of options because I wasn't sure what you liked, so there should be enough for you all for a couple of days. Don't worry, I didn't cook them, so they're safe to eat. The green bag has coffee courtesy of Wicker Hill Café, which I swear will make all your worries disappear if only for the duration of each sip. There are also enough scones to feed an army, which was Sophie's doing. Oh, and cookies and chocolate, which is my doing. Anyway, I hope your weekend is better than your week, and I'm a message away if you need anything. Ruth (and Piglet).

CHAPTER FIVE

*H*ow *do you feel about being my tour guide today?*
The message that awaited Ruth when she woke suddenly made her Sunday look far more promising.

It would be my pleasure. Want to begin the tour at the café around 9?

That would leave Ruth enough time to grab a quick shower, but not too much time to overthink about the fact that this would be her first official date with Ollie. Sophie had taken the day off at the café, so they would avoid an interrogation. Plus, they could start the day with coffee, which was a win-win. The short walk to the main street seemed infinitely longer as Ruth's stomach filled with nervous butterflies.

Ollie was sporting much more casual black linen pants and a soft knit cardigan today. Ruth took in the view of Ollie standing to the side of the café, in conversation with none other than Ruth's aunt. Greta had been gone from the cottage already when Ruth left, and apparently, they had the same idea. Ruth bit her lip nervously as she made her way toward them. She hoped Greta wasn't interrogating her date.

"Hey, you two," Ruth said as they both turned toward her.

"Hi, honey. I came out to grab a bite with Marjorie and bumped into Olivia here. You didn't mention you had plans together today."

Greta gave her the same look as before, the one that conveyed so much without saying a word. The one that made it clear she wasn't happy with the lack of information Ruth was providing to her.

"I didn't. We didn't. I mean—"

"I only texted Ruth this morning to ask her to be my tour guide, so it's very last-minute plans on my part. Henry seems to be doing a little better, so my sister kicked me out of the house. She was sick of my hovering."

Ruth was thankful for Ollie's smooth explanation, which was a contrast to her babbling response.

"Make sure you stop by the cottage on your tour. I'm headed out for the afternoon, but I can leave a few snacks there for lunch. Enjoy yourselves."

The wink Greta shot her was a surprise to Ruth. Her quick acceptance of Ollie was a good sign. Ruth had been sure that Greta would be as hesitant about Ollie as the rest of the village seemed to be, given their adoration of Mr B. and Ollie's absence. But there wasn't a hint of judgement coming from Greta, and Ruth felt bad for underestimating her. She gave her aunt a quick hug before she turned to Ollie.

"Have you eaten?" Ruth asked.

Ollie shook her head no as her eyes took Ruth in slowly. It sent a shiver up Ruth's spine, and her cheeks heated at the soft smile of approval that appeared on Ollie's face.

"Then let's grab some takeaway coffee and muffins for breakfast. We can eat them over at the park on our first stop."

After they grabbed the to go bag, Ruth adopted her tour guide persona.

"To the left of us you'll find the place where I scratched my knee a week after moving here, and became best friends with Sophie," Ruth said, with a flourish of her hand.

"Were those two things related?" Ollie asked.

Ruth nodded as she sipped her coffee and led them toward the small playground. "Yup. My aunt brought me for a walk after finally coaxing me out of the house. My anxiety already had its grips on me then. I don't know if it was something I struggled with before the move, but I don't really remember a time where I didn't. I remember not wanting to leave the cottage, but finally I gave in. Greta was horrified when I tripped over my own feet and landed right on my left knee, scratching it pretty badly."

Ollie winced but Ruth smiled, because luckily that wasn't the part of the story that stood out in her head.

"Sophie's family have always run the café and she saw what happened from the window. She came running over with a far-too-big bandage and a wad of napkins. The bandage was useless for the graze, but it made me laugh, which is something my aunt has been forever grateful to Sophie for. That was the start of our friendship."

They sat on a bench inside the walls of the small green area. The playground itself had some really nice new equipment from a fundraiser where the whole village chipped in. It was often filled midweek with kids from the local crèche and preschool. On an early Sunday morning, though, it was almost empty, apart from one woman chasing a toddler around the small swing set.

"It sounds like the start of a beautiful friendship," Ollie said.

Ollie angled herself toward Ruth, and Ruth copied her movements. She pulled the muffins from the bag and passed one to Ollie, laughing as Ollie moaned in appreciation at the first bite.

"This seriously rivals the coffee and I never thought anything could compare. You have good taste in friends," Ollie said.

Ruth nodded as she swallowed her own mouthful and licked a crumb from her lips.

"They have a small selection, but all are amazing in their own right. They even do a decent online trade for the coffee now, since Sophie took over. I took some product photos, and she got a website set up and it took off. She only opens for orders sporadically, which makes it all that more appealing."

"She's smart. Keep people wanting, it works wonders," Ollie said with a slight grin.

Ruth's stomach flipped from the words. It was so natural sitting here with Ollie, as if it was just a regular extension of their daily conversations that had been building to this moment. Ruth pulled out her phone and took a photo of them, then laughed at the result. Ollie had taken a bite of food right before Ruth captured the image which captured the moment perfectly.

"Finish up, we've got a lot to see. I don't take my tour guide duties lightly," Ruth said.

Ollie laughed and finished the muffin, savouring the last bite.

"I promise you'll get to taste it again." Ruth chuckled.

"I'm holding you to that," Ollie replied.

Ruth brought them back down the main street, pointing out different places and memories from throughout the years. Her tour didn't consist so much of buildings and landmarks, but more of people and stories. She brought them down the path toward her favourite spot, the river she had sent Ollie a photo of.

"This is the best place on my tour. I love it here," Ruth said.

She plopped down on the riverbank with a happy sigh and ran her fingers through the soft grass.

"I can see why. It's peaceful," Ollie said, as she sat down beside her.

"That's part of it, yes," Ruth replied with a nod.

"And the other part?"

"Rivers are ever changing. I hate change."

Ollie frowned and tilted her head as if to try making sense of the words.

"Anxiety and change don't go well together. It's actually part of how I got into photography. I take photos of things so I can see the changes happen bit by bit, so I can notice the subtleties, and not wake up one day to everything different. But rivers are always changing. The water is constantly flowing. The river we're looking at now isn't the same as the one I saw yesterday, or the day before. It's consistent in its inconsistency. It's comforting. I probably sound silly but—"

Ollie placed a hand over Ruth's where it lay on the grass, and Ruth lifted her gaze to meet Ollie's.

"It's not silly. It makes perfect sense. Thank you for sharing that with me," Ollie said softly.

Ruth gulped as her mouth became suddenly dry. The soft lapping of the flowing water faded into a dull background noise as she dropped her eyes to Ollie's lips and then back up again. Ollie leaned in slowly and gave plenty of time for Ruth to pull back. Which was something that Ruth had no intention of doing. Ruth's eyes fluttered shut as the warmth of Ollie's breath tickled her lips. Her brain was screaming for the contact to come, and when it did, everything else disappeared.

Ollie's lips were as soft as they looked. Ruth deepened the kiss and before she knew it, they were making out like teenagers who were savouring every moment, as if afraid to get caught. Ollie's fingers were in Ruth's hair as she pulled them closer, and Ruth got lost in the varying sensations flying through her body. Ollie slowed her movements and Ruth followed suit, until their passionate kisses turned to soft pecks. Which was far more appropriate for their public location.

"Wow," Ollie whispered softly as her lips continued to find Ruth's like they were pulled together by a magnetic force. *Wow indeed.*

❖

Olivia's lips still tingled as Ruth led her hand-in-hand down a winding dirt path. She was still floating on the high of the kiss and was sure she'd follow Ruth anywhere in that moment. Ruth's thumb brushed in a soft back and forth motion over Olivia's hand as they walked in companionable silence. As they rounded a corner, the familiar cottage from Ruth's photograph appeared ahead.

"It looks even more magical in real life," Olivia said.

"It has its moments," Ruth replied, but the proud smile she sported showed her agreement.

As they walked through the front door, Ruth's dog bounded its way over to sniff Olivia out.

"Pig, down, girl." Ruth tried to stop the dog from jumping on her, but Olivia was having none of it. She got down on her knees and let the dog nuzzle her in the way dogs did best.

"Hey there, beautiful girl. You're just trying to say hi, aren't you? You're a good girl." Olivia gave Piglet all of her attention for a moment, which included mandatory belly rubs when the dog rolled over. She looked up to see Ruth watching them with a smile. "I'm not gonna lie. Her photo on your dating profile was the deciding factor for messaging, you know. I had to thank her."

Ruth chuckled and called Piglet over to her bed. With one final lick of Olivia's hand, the dog made her way over and curled up. Ruth gave her a quick rub and then stage whispered, "Thank you."

As they both washed their hands in the kitchen sink, Olivia took in the interior of the cottage. It was an open plan kitchen and living space, which was almost exactly how she pictured it being. Every available shelf space was covered in books.

"I knew you liked books, but I didn't know you collected every possible book you could get your hands on." Olivia widened her eyes in mock surprise.

"I do love books. But most of these are actually Greta's. I don't even notice it anymore—it's always been covered in books."

Ruth gestured to the small table and grabbed some food from the fridge. She fixed a platter of various snacks for them to share and brought it to the table.

"This looks great and all, but I thought I was getting toasted cheese and Taytos when I finally got to the fairy-tale cottage. Bit of a letdown," Olivia joked.

Ruth slid into the chair across from her as she set the food between them.

"It's not dinner time, Ollie," Ruth deadpanned. Olivia laughed at the serious look on Ruth's face before an adorable smile broke through.

"Guess you'll just have to invite me back. Is it a candlelight dinner? Paired with Capri Sun? Or do we eat them in a blanket fort watching cartoons? Either way I'm down," Olivia teased with a shrug of her shoulders.

"You're kidding, but that sounds like an impressive date to me. Candlelight dinners are for real world dates, not fairy tales," Ruth replied.

"Who said I was kidding? I would never joke about a Capri Sun."

They ate in silence for a moment as Olivia's head filled

with so many questions she had to get some out. She found herself wanting to know everything about Ruth.

"How long have you lived here?" Olivia was hesitant to ask, but it had been the question at the forefront of her mind again since their earlier conversation.

"Is that okay to ask? I was just wondering when you mentioned moving here. It must've been weird moving to a village as small as this as a kid," Olivia said.

"It was. My memories are vague of that time. I was six, and I'd just lost both my parents, so although moving to a tiny village was weird, it was sort of just another part of the weird turn my life had taken, you know?" Ruth replied.

Olivia reached across the table and placed her hand in Ruth's briefly.

"I'm so sorry about your parents. That must have been tough. And still is, I'm sure."

Ruth squeezed Olivia's hand where it lay in hers before she began to butter some freshly made scones and passed half to Olivia.

"It was, is. It's sort of hard to describe. I don't remember a lot about them. I love my aunt and I love living here. So, it always feels weird when I consider that my life could've gone a totally different direction. I'm obviously not glad about the circumstances that brought me here, but I also know how lucky I am. I live in a fairy-tale cottage—how can I complain?"

Ruth's smile didn't quite meet her eyes. Olivia caught the struggle in her words, like a script Ruth had rehearsed to herself.

"It is pretty idyllic here. But two things can be true. You can be grateful for your life and people here, and sad for what you lost." Olivia spoke softly, worried she was overstepping. Ruth was silent for a moment and Olivia was about to apologize when Ruth finally spoke.

"You're right. I've been working on that in therapy. I still have a way to go on my journey with detangling my feelings about it all. I don't discuss it much with anyone. Greta doesn't really talk about my parents, I assume because she's worried it would upset me, but it created this sort of secrecy around them, too."

Olivia nodded. She could relate to that to an extent. "It's not the same thing, but when Henry first left, my mom sort of did that, too. She didn't talk about him, and so I stopped asking. I was afraid to upset her, and she was probably afraid of the same, and we were both focused on taking care of my sister, who was so young. His name became sort of like this space between us that we were both afraid to breach."

Ruth nodded in understanding. "I remember bits and pieces. Our house was much bigger. There was a large back garden and it had so many toys, like almost as much as a playground. Or at least, that's how it felt when I was six. I remember it because it was so different when I got here. The cottage was so much smaller, and there were no fences around the garden. No swing sets or big toys."

Ruth seemed lost in her memories as she spoke, and although the topic wasn't a particularly happy one, Olivia couldn't help but smile at the daydream look on Ruth's face.

"It was so different. Wicker Hill sort of became my playground after a while. I realized I didn't need fences to keep me safe here, because the people around me did that job well. There was nowhere I could explore that someone wouldn't know Greta. It was kind of like one big, eccentric family."

Olivia chuckled, knowing from only a short time in Wicker Hill that Ruth's description was accurate.

"My imagination had no limits around here. I climbed trees and played in the river. I read many, many books lying beside the riverbed or under the big tree out back. The cottage that had felt so tiny when I first arrived made me feel so comforted, knowing my aunt was never too far. We watched movies and Greta read stories to me and slowly it became home. The only home I remember, if I'm honest."

Ruth's voice, which had been lively when retelling getting to know Wicker Hill, became wistful at the end.

"Does it bother you, not knowing more?" Olivia asked.

"Sometimes. I know what they look like. But I don't remember what they sound like. I don't really remember what our house looked like. I don't know if they read me stories, or what memories I have of them are true or made up over the years. Like if I got my sense of humour from one of them, or my laugh. Or my anxiety, for that matter. Sometimes I wonder if they had any friends or neighbours who wonder about me, you know? I was there and then just gone. Surely someone in their life cared enough to wonder what happened to me."

Olivia wondered what happened to them, but it wasn't the right time to ask if Ruth hadn't offered it yet.

"Those are all understandable things to think about. Would Greta know? I know she hasn't talked about them much, but you could ask," Ollie said.

Ruth shrugged and moved to clear off their plates as Olivia got up to help her.

"That's the thing. I don't remember Greta. Like, before they died. I do remember that when she came to bring me back here, she was someone I didn't know. But my mom was her sister, so how could that be? We don't even live a million miles apart. They lived on the south side of the city so it's what, a couple hours' drive max?"

"Oh, that's where I grew up. Where my mom still lives, actually. Yeah, it's a couple hours from here. Maybe there's a valid explanation, though. You won't know unless you ask."

It wasn't totally strange that Olivia and Ruth grew up

not far from each other for the first few years of their lives, considering how small the county was. But it was weird to think they could have walked past each other or been to the same places as kids.

"I just figured if it was something Greta thought I would want to know, she'd have told me, right? I don't know. Anyway, where has the time gone? I better continue your tour before it gets too dark. You still haven't seen my favourite tree."

Ruth wagged her eyebrows and turned to grab her bag, but the slumping of her shoulders made it clear that the conversation had weighed on her. So, although Olivia still had so much she wanted to know, she followed Ruth's lead.

"I must see this tree, or the tour will be deemed a failure," Ollie said.

Ruth shot her a grateful smile and they made their way outside, leaving the conversation behind in the small fairy-tale cottage.

CHAPTER SIX

It had been three days since her first date with Ollie, and Ruth hadn't been able to stop thinking about it. For some good reasons, and other not so great ones. She spent time reminiscing about their kiss in vivid detail. It was definitely one she wanted to repeat and had awoken a hunger in Ruth that left her aching in so many ways. Then her thoughts would inevitably veer toward their conversation at the cottage. She hadn't spoken to anyone so candidly about her feelings around her parents and Wicker Hill, not even Sophie.

Home. That's how she had explained it to Ollie, that Wicker Hill was the only home she remembered, and it was true. But even that didn't encompass the full confusing mixture of feelings that the word brought up for her. If her parents had survived the fire like she had, what would home be like right now? A big house in the suburbs, most likely. Would she have siblings, pets, friends? Everything good in her life right now was here in Wicker Hill. The thought of never knowing this quirky little town with its overprotective, but full of love, residents was beyond Ruth's comprehension.

She grappled with something that had plagued her for as long as she could remember—the thought that being happy and comfortable here, and calling it home, meant she was happy her parents weren't alive. It flitted through her head anytime her anxious brain got too quiet. The first time she had uttered the sentence to a therapist when she originally sought help for her anxiety, the therapist had listened and then explained how untrue the statement was. That it was irrational, and finding peace in the life she had been given didn't negate what she lost.

That had been the first time she quit therapy. Ruth didn't need to pay someone to tell her that her thoughts were irrational, she did that for herself well enough. The knowledge that they were illogical didn't stop the thoughts from crowding her brain when she least expected it. Ruth had eventually gone back to therapy, and it was an amazing tool for her anxiety as a whole. But she had yet to make peace with the conflicting feelings around what home meant to her, past and present.

"There seem to be a lot of thoughts wrapped up in that head of yours, honey. Want to spill some of them?"

Greta placed a hand on Ruth's head as she came up behind where Ruth sat on their worn-in couch. Ruth leaned her head back and smiled at Greta in what she hoped resembled reassurance. Greta's eyes said she wasn't buying it. She raised an eyebrow and then moved toward the kitchen. Ruth chewed on her lip for a moment before she spoke hesitantly.

"I was just thinking…about my parents."

If Ruth hadn't been paying close attention, she would've missed the slight pause to Greta's steps.

"Anything in particular brought this up for you?"

Greta's voice was the same as usual, but the lightness seemed more forced. That, or Ruth was paranoid, which was also a definite possibility.

"Ollie asked about when I moved here when we were together on Sunday, so I guess it's just been in my head since," Ruth said.

Greta nodded for a moment as she cracked some eggs into a bowl.

"How'd the date, I mean *tour*, go?" Greta asked.

She shot Ruth a wink as she continued preparing scrambled eggs for breakfast, and Ruth frowned. No, it wasn't her imagination. Greta was avoiding the topic.

"It was good. Why don't you want to talk about them?"

Ruth blurted the words before she had too much time to consider them. Greta continued with the breakfast preparation as if nothing was out of the ordinary.

"About your parents? We can talk about them if you want, I was just interested to hear about your date. It's been a while since I've seen you smitten with anyone."

Ruth groaned as her face heated. "I am not smitten," she mumbled.

Sophie walked through the door right at that moment, and if Ruth didn't know better, she would've sworn Greta had magically produced her.

"Totally smitten. You can lie to yourself, my love, but you can't lie to us. Is that scrambled eggs I smell? I'm starving."

Sophie tapped Ruth's head in much the same fashion that Greta had, before bypassing her to head to the kitchen.

"Don't you own a café that you happen to live above, that has plenty of food?" Ruth said right at the same time as her aunt chimed in.

"There's plenty for everyone. Grab two plates and set the table. I have to get a move on anyway, I forgot there's an early appointment I need to get set up for."

Ruth uncharacteristically glared at her aunt's retreating form as Greta left the bowl of freshly made scrambled egg on the counter and dashed off in a hurry.

"What was that all about?" Sophie asked around a spoonful of the egg that was already on its way to her mouth.

"You noticed, too? She's being weird, right?" Ruth said.

Sophie set about serving the eggs for them both as Ruth made her way over to the table and poured them orange juice.

"No, not her. You. I haven't seen you give a death glare like that since sixth class sports day when Anna McLoughlin won the egg and spoon race after tripping you before the finish line," Sophie said.

"Well, it was a clear violation of the rules, she should've been disqualified," Ruth huffed.

"Yeah, yeah, you were robbed. But anyway, what did Greta do to deserve the glare?"

Ruth weighed up what to say and eventually just went with the truth, or what little of it she knew anyway.

"I brought up my parents and she just totally changed the subject," Ruth said.

Sophie tilted her head as if to take Ruth in before she replied.

"By the glare and the look on your face right now, I'm guessing it wasn't due to her rushing to work?"

Ruth shook her head.

"She wasn't rushing when she got up. Not until I mentioned my parents, and then I asked her why she never wants to talk about them."

"What did she say to that?" Sophie asked.

"She didn't say anything really. She was trying to distract me with talking about seeing me smitten about Ollie, and well, that's when you walked in and heard the rest. Suddenly she has to leave for work an hour earlier than usual."

Ruth couldn't even taste most of the food she was spooning into her mouth. Her thoughts were getting more and more exaggerated by the minute.

"I don't get it. Did she hate them? Is that what it's about?

Even if they didn't get on, surely she could find one or two nice things to tell me about them. I don't know why it's never bothered me this much before. But she's never told me *anything*."

Tears pricked at the corner of Ruth's eyes, and she could feel the tightness growing in her chest. She took some deep breaths, in through her nose and out through her mouth, and touched her thumb to each of her fingers in a pattern she'd been using for years now to calm herself.

"I don't know why, Ruthie. I do know that Greta adores you. And I know she wants what's best for you. So, whatever her reasoning, I'm sure in her mind it's in your best interests."

Sophie's words were meant to console her, but they only added to the fast-growing anger.

"That's the problem. She's deciding what's in *my* best interests. I'm not a little kid anymore that she needs to protect. I'm an adult and I deserve to be treated like one. You're my person, Soph. Be mad with me, don't be rational and defend her."

Sophie banged the table so hard it startled Ruth, and she sat up straight.

"Damn that woman, damn her to hell." Sophie threw her head back and yelled the words in a dramatic voice that had Ruth bursting into shocked laughter.

"What, too much?" Sophie asked, with a casual shrug. "I know you're pissed, and maybe you have reason to be. If you want me to be mad, I'll be mad. Whatever you need. But, and don't kill me for saying it, maybe Greta deserves the tiniest amount of benefit of the doubt here? It might have been a shock for her to hear you bring them up. Let her ruminate a little and try again. If she still fobs you off, then I'll be behind you in the madness one hundred percent."

Ruth nodded, even if she didn't think shock was what held Greta back from the conversation. The more she considered things fully, the more she remembered similar distraction techniques whenever she had brought the topic up before.

"Thanks. But we both know you won't actually get mad at Greta," Ruth said.

Sophie shrugged nonchalantly. "What can I say? I'm a sucker for an older lady."

Ruth sighed at Sophie's words and accompanying grin.

"Stop fangirling over my aunt, Soph. It wasn't cool when we were kids and it's less cool now," Ruth said.

"Not my fault you got the hot gay aunt. I definitely thought finding out I was a girl all those years ago would give me a shot with her, but alas, I must pine from afar." Sophie exaggerated a pout and wiped a fake tear from her eye.

When they were teenagers, and Sophie confided in Ruth that she was a girl and always had been, Ruth never doubted it for a second. Sophie was Sophie, even before Ruth knew to call her that.

"Listen my love, joking aside, my crush on Greta has everything to do with the fact that she cares so deeply about you, and everyone. I'll forever be grateful for the support she gave me, that both of you did, and yes, that may bias me a little here. I'm your person, always, but part of that means reminding you that your aunt has given you so much. So maybe give her a little time."

Ruth hated when Sophie spoke sense while Ruth was filled with emotions, but she was right. The least that Greta deserved from Ruth was the benefit of the doubt, and she would give her that. But one way or another, she needed answers, sooner rather than later.

❖

The doorbell rang and snapped Olivia out of the daze she had been in. A daze filled with the memories of her lips pressed against Ruth's, and fantasies of many more areas Olivia wanted to explore. The doorbell sent another shrill reminder of the intrusion to her daydreams, and Olivia got up to make her way to the front door.

"Hello, dear, hope I'm not bothering you. Is your father awake?"

A woman Olivia vaguely recognized from her few trips into the village bustled her way into the house without waiting for an invite. Olivia furrowed her brow and stood holding the open door as the woman turned to look at her expectantly.

"Well, close that door now before you leave all the heat out. Is he in his room? I can head on up."

Olivia shut the door and shook her head to wake herself up from whatever trance she was in that enabled this woman to get this far without question.

"Wait, sorry, who are you? I mean, you're a friend of Henry's, I assume?" Olivia asked.

She moved toward the woman and subtly blocked the way to the stairs that led to Henry's room.

"I'm Breda Guiney. Most of the young ones around here call me Mrs Guiney, the ones with manners, anyway. I worked at the local post office with your dad since the day he moved here, what, fifteen years ago now?"

"I'm—"

"And you're Livvie, right? He talks about you a lot. It's good to *finally* meet you."

The last sentence held an edge that sent a bristle down Olivia's spine. Clearly, this woman had already painted a picture from whatever Henry had said about the type of daughter Olivia was. The type whom she hadn't met in the fifteen years of knowing Olivia's father.

"Olivia, actually. My friends call me Ollie."

Olivia held out her hand and tacked on a smile for good measure. Whatever this woman thought of her, Olivia wouldn't give her the satisfaction of living up to it. Mrs Guiney shook her hand quickly, all the while looking over Olivia's shoulder toward the stairs.

"I'll just get past you then, Olivia."

She went to move to the side and Olivia mimicked her actions. She didn't want to make a bad impression, but Grace had warned her before she left that people would make themselves quite at home here. She had made it clear to Olivia that the only way to keep it from becoming overwhelming was to set firm boundaries.

"I'm sorry, Mrs Guiney, but Henry's asleep at the moment. He's been in quite a bit of pain, and Dr Hegarty isn't long gone. The painkillers will keep him out for another few hours yet. If you want to give a call first in future, I'll let you know a good time to come around so you aren't wasting a trip."

Olivia softened her words with another smile but held firm. Mrs Guiney looked taken aback as if Olivia had personally offended her.

"I know you're new around here, my dear, but we've all been looking after your *father*. He'll want to see me, and he loves hearing the village news. I know everything that goes on around here, you see, and I give him his updates every week."

Olivia took a breath to calm herself and closed her eyes for a brief moment. She was sure that this woman had Henry's best interests at heart, regardless of how she felt about Olivia. But right now, it was Olivia's job to care for her patient, and part of that meant protecting him from other people who thought they knew what was best. A job she was well used to working in the hospital. Friends, and even family, were clouded by emotion and feelings including their own wants and needs. There was no room for that when treating a sick patient.

"I'll tell him you dropped by, and as I said, give the landline a ring tomorrow and I can let you know the best time to drop by to make sure Henry is up to the visit."

Olivia walked toward the front door and held it open before adding, "I'm sure he'll appreciate the news a lot more when he's awake to hear it."

Mrs Guiney looked between the stairs and the door and back again. Olivia wondered if she was calculating the likelihood of making it up the stairs before Olivia tackled her. Olivia hoped her eyes were conveying the fact that she would, in fact, resort to that, if need be. She was nothing if not stubborn.

"Well, I'll be by tomorrow, then. I hope you're taking good care of him. He's very loved around here, you know."

Oh, I definitely know, Olivia thought, as Mrs Guiney made her way out the door.

"Be sure to call first!" Olivia said after her in an enthusiastic tone that sounded as fake as the smile she dropped the minute the door shut. She pressed her back against the closed door and sighed as her shoulders dropped. Olivia was exhausted, and dealing with all the people who loved this new and improved version of Henry didn't help. Except this version of him wasn't new at all. The version Olivia remembered was even older, a fact she still hadn't found a way to deal with. She grabbed her phone from the seat she had been quietly resting on before the intrusion and typed out a quick text to Ruth.

How close are you to Mrs Guiney?

The dots that appeared almost immediately brought a genuine smile to Olivia's face as she flopped back into the chair.

Oh, no. What did she do this time? Her lack of tact is well known throughout the village, to everyone but her it seems.

Olivia chuckled. At least it wasn't just her, which was a relief. She was a little worried about setting a bad tone with everyone in the village that had practically raised Ruth. It wouldn't look good for their future. *Our future.* The thought made Olivia pause as her fingers hovered over the screen to type her reply. Was a future even on the cards?

With Ruth living back in Wicker Hill, and Olivia returning to the city in a few weeks, how viable was it that they'd continue what they started? Olivia chastised herself as she remembered that they had only been on one date. They had only had one kiss. She was jumping much too far ahead, and that was never a good idea. She deleted the few words of her reply message and pressed the call button instead, not unaware of the calm that surrounded her the minute she heard Ruth's voice.

CHAPTER SEVEN

F ancy meeting you here."

Ruth slid into the empty seat across from Ollie at the café and wrapped her hands around the warm mug. It was a cold, dry morning and Ruth was grateful for the heater set up beside the outdoor table. She pointed down at the muffin that Ollie had already begun eating.

"I told you you'd get to taste it again," Ruth said.

"You did. I wondered if I had exaggerated the deliciousness in my head, but nope, it's still just as good," Ollie replied.

Ruth smiled and reached out to grab a piece from the plate before popping it into her mouth. She laughed at the shocked look Ollie shot her.

"This is not the kind of food you share. I'll buy you one—hell, I'll buy you a dozen, but this is mine." Ollie wrapped her arms around the remaining piece of muffin on the plate and fixed a serious look on her face.

Ruth slowly licked the last crumb from her lip as Ollie's eyes took in the action. Her serious expression filled with a different kind of hunger that sent a thrill through Ruth.

"No sharing, even with me?" Ruth batted her eyelashes and did her best version of puppy dog eyes.

"Not fair," Ollie mumbled as she released her fortress around the muffin.

"All's fair in love and muffins." Ruth grinned as she snuck her hand out again and inched it toward the plate. Ollie reached out and covered Ruth's hand with her own. Before Ruth could protest, Ollie picked up the last piece of muffin and held it out to Ruth. The food pressed against Ruth's lips, and they parted for Ollie's fingers while Ruth's eyes never left Ollie's. The heat had turned up several notches and Ollie's lips parted as if in response. Ruth was frozen in the moment that had turned from teasing to longing, until the clang of a plate snapped her out of it.

"On the house, before my café gets shut down for indecent exposure."

Ruth blinked and looked up at Sophie, then down at the second muffin Sophie had placed between them on the table. Ruth looked across to Ollie, whose face was now a deep shade of red.

"How about you take it to go and get a room?" Sophie shot over her shoulder as she walked back to the counter. Ruth shook her head at Sophie's retreating form before focusing her attention on Ollie again. Ollie's cheeks were showing no sign of returning to their regular colour, and Ruth couldn't help the laugh that bubbled up.

Ollie dropped her head into her hands and groaned, "I'm mortified."

Ruth wiped a stray tear from her eye as her laughter subsided. "It's just Sophie. She's jealous I'm the one being fed by the hot nurse."

Now it was Ruth's turn to go red as the heat crept up her neck.

Ollie raised her head and grinned. "Hot nurse, hmm?"

Ruth shrugged and tried to ignore her heated face. She refused to shy away from Ollie's gaze.

"Yup. What can I say? I have a thing for women in uniform," Ruth said.

Ollie's eyes widened in surprise and Ruth's stomach flipped at the lust reflected in them. Ollie's phone beeped and she glanced down at it, then stood.

"I have to get back. I only managed to grab some time because the doctor was with Henry. He just messaged to say he's done, so I better get going," Ollie said.

Ruth stood with her, and Ollie reached out to squeeze her hand.

"I'm glad I ran into you," Ruth said. She was unsure how to appropriately say goodbye to someone you were kind of dating, without officially calling it that, who took up most of the space in your head.

Ollie hesitated for a moment, but then leaned in and brushed a soft kiss against Ruth's cheek. Before pulling back, she whispered softly, "I didn't bring my uniform, but maybe if you're lucky I'll dig out a photo or two."

The words alone were almost enough to make Ruth melt, but the wink Ollie shot before she walked out had Ruth scrambling to sit on the chair again before her legs gave out. She absentmindedly picked at the muffin in front of her as Ollie walked away. Ruth's gaze was on Ollie until she rounded the corner out of eyeline.

"You two need to fuck before the whole village gets a show."

Sophie sat across from Ruth in the newly unoccupied seat.

"Shut up!" Ruth whispered harshly, glancing around the thankfully empty street.

"Seriously. The waves of heat radiating from between you both almost melted *me*. I'm surprised you didn't burst into flames," Sophie said.

Ruth couldn't argue with that. She was surprised she hadn't, too. The molten pool gathered between her legs was proof enough of the effect Ollie had on her.

"Is it the weekend yet?" Ruth sighed and Sophie laughed.

"Two more days, my love. Do you have a grand plan for date number two?"

Ruth shook her head. She didn't want to wait two days. But she wanted them to enjoy their second date peacefully, and that meant waiting until Grace got back. They had loosely agreed to meet Saturday, but so far that was the extent of a plan.

"I can't exactly bring her back to my tiny cottage with the paper-thin walls for a night of passion, can I? And her place isn't exactly the prime setting for romance either. This village needs a goddamn B&B."

Sophie smiled and patted Ruth's hand gently.

"There, there, my poor sex starved friend. I'm not sure pitching a B&B in a town of a couple hundred people is going to solve your problems. However, what might do that is the knowledge that Greta is going to be occupied until at least midnight on Saturday with the pub quiz. The one you should really be going to, that I assume you forgot about."

"Shit." Ruth had totally blanked on the yearly fundraiser Greta organized for the animal shelter she volunteered at. The local pub put on a quiz and Greta organized a raffle and prizes. Ruth suddenly felt like a terrible niece.

"I have to go. Ugh. I already paid for a table for our team," Ruth groaned.

Their team consisted of Ruth, Sophie, Sophie's brother, and his girlfriend. They were currently the undefeated champions of the pub quiz four years running.

"Luckily for you I have someone to fill your spot. I'm sure Greta won't mind when you explain that I asked you to give up your place so I could bring my date, like the good supportive friend you are."

"Wait, since when do you have a date? Why am I only hearing about this now?"

Sophie shrugged and got up to serve the two women who had walked into the café.

"You're not getting away that easily, I need details," Ruth yelled after her.

"All in good time, my love. Now scoot, I only have two tables out here and you've been occupying one with a free muffin for too long. Go focus on your own budding love life and we'll discuss mine later."

Ruth's curiosity was on high alert. Sophie was rarely cagey with her romantic interests. Ruth usually knew about them before the object of Sophie's attention did. For Sophie to have a date without Ruth even knowing someone was on the horizon? Unheard of. But the café was starting to pick up with the early lunch crowd, so Ruth took her leave. She walked home with a new excitement bubbling at the potential of an evening alone with Ollie in two days.

❖

"Have you talked to him much?" Grace asked as she put a spoon full of sugary cereal into her mouth. Olivia sat across from her at the dining room table as she ate her own, far less fun, breakfast of toast. Grace had arrived back less than an hour ago, and like the weekend before, they chatted about the week's updates over breakfast.

"No, I completely ignore him all day long," Olivia retorted.

"You know what I mean. Have you talked to him like he's your father and not a patient?"

Olivia took a bite of her toast and chewed slowly. She was buying herself some time to manage her words. Grace knew better than to ask that, and part of Olivia suspected that her sister was looking for a fairy-tale ending to a tragic story.

"He's spent most of the time sleeping. The new medication seems to be helping with the pain but it's knocking him out," Olivia said.

Grace sighed. Olivia's deflection had clearly not gone unnoticed.

"He's a good person, Livvie. I know you know that. Don't you think he deserves—"

Olivia held up her hand to cut Grace off.

"Let's not get into a conversation about what anyone deserves, okay? I came here for you. I am taking damn good care of him. Better than any facility I could have paid to do so. I am doing this because it is what you want and need, not out of any obligation because he and I share blood. That's enough."

Grace nodded and Olivia saw the tears gathered in the corner of her eyes. Olivia closed her eyes and took a deep breath, steeling herself against her own emotions threatening beneath the surface. She could talk the talk all she wanted, but Olivia couldn't hide the truth from herself.

"I'm sorry, Gracie. I know you love him. I am taking good care of him, I promise."

Olivia reached across the table and held Grace's hand in hers. She could never stand seeing her sister upset and hated being the cause of it even more.

"I know you are. I'm not saying it just for him, Livvie. I don't want you to have any regrets when…there's not much time."

The tears fell down Grace's cheeks at the last part and Olivia moved to her. She wrapped her arms around Grace and held her closely while she sobbed, stroking her hair and rocking her gently, like she used to when Grace was little.

"I'm here for you. That's the important thing to me, Gracie."

As Grace's tears subsided, Olivia sat back down. She held her own tears inside. They could wait for the quiet of her room.

"I heard you met Mrs Guiney."

A small grin broke out on Grace's tear-stained face as Olivia groaned loudly.

"You could've warned me, you brat," Olivia huffed.

"I told you, people like to make themselves at home in this village. She's harmless, really. And she loves Dad. I think she kind of took him under her wing when he first got here, almost like a son. You know he never knew his own mom."

Olivia wracked her brain. *Had* she known that? It seemed like new information, but surely it was something she should've known, right? Both her grandparents from Henry's side were dead, but she couldn't recall specifics around them at all.

"He never knew her, like at all?" Olivia asked.

Grace nodded as she finished the food in her mouth before responding.

"Yeah, she died not long after he was born. And his dad was not exactly the warm and comforting parental figure," Grace sneered, "so I think maybe she was sort of a stand-in parent. Obviously, he was an adult when he moved here, but adult or not…I think she gave him something he was missing his whole life. So, she may be a bit much to deal with, but she's good for him."

Olivia nodded in response, but her head was processing a lot of what Grace said. She had spent so much of her adult life actively trying to not think of Henry that she forgot he was a person with his own life before he became her father.

"Speaking of which, I've actually asked her to pop by later and be here with Dad while we're out," Grace said.

"We? I thought when we spoke during the week you said you were staying in while I went out with Ruth?"

Grace shrugged and got up to bring her bowl to the sink. If Olivia didn't know better, she would think Grace was avoiding looking at her.

"I got invited to a thing in the village. It's just some fundraiser that's on every year, so I figured it might be good to go."

That confirmed it, Grace was definitely avoiding looking. There was more to this for sure, but what that could be was escaping Olivia.

"You go. I can stay here and keep an eye on him. He'll need his meds and—"

"You're going," Grace interjected.

Olivia was taken aback by the force in Grace's words as she spun around to face her.

"I'm serious. You need to get out of this house, Livvie. Up until a couple weeks ago we survived here without you." Olivia went to interrupt but Grace held a hand up before she could get a word out. "I'm not finished. I am beyond grateful we don't have to now, and you being here has made all of the difference. But Mrs Guiney has stayed with Dad before, and she knows what he needs. You've also made a far too detailed list to go along with it. You need a night off, and if you don't take it, then I'm not going."

Olivia nodded, and it hit her in that moment how much her little sister had grown. Grace was a full-grown adult now. It shouldn't be a surprise to Olivia, but somehow it was.

"Well, first you need a shower. Then you need to take yourself out of this house and go kiss that girlfriend of yours. I don't want to see you until I'm leaving tomorrow," Grace said.

"Hold up. I never told you Ruth was my girlfriend, and where exactly do you expect me to sleep tonight? I'm just going out for a few hours."

Grace sighed and walked forward. She reached up to put a hand on Olivia's shoulder.

"Dear sister, you really do not understand small villages at all, do you? I know everything. Including the fact that *your girlfriend* may have an empty cottage tonight that I'm sure you'll find a way to make use of, so like I said, I'll see you tomorrow."

Grace smiled sweetly at Olivia's open-mouthed face before turning and walking out of the room. Despite the shock of her little sister knowing more about her date than she did, all Olivia could focus on was how good the words *your girlfriend* sounded to her ears.

CHAPTER EIGHT

R uth checked the clock on her phone for the tenth time in ten minutes, pacing back and forth across the small hallway leading from the cottage door to the living room. Ollie was late. Only by eight minutes, which was barely notable in most situations. But as the minutes ticked by and Ruth paced, her brain was filled with every worst-case scenario imaginable. It was interesting how many overlapping images her mind could conjure up given the opportunity.

Greta had left an hour ago, after much reassurance that she wasn't upset with Ruth for not attending the quiz tonight. She casually mentioned that she wanted to have a few drinks at the quiz and not worry about getting home, so her friend had offered the spare room to Greta for the night since she lived beside the pub. Greta shot Ruth a wink while she went out the door, which confirmed there was nothing casual about the arrangement at all. Greta was making sure Ruth knew they would have the cottage to themselves, and that alone was disconcerting enough.

Was Ruth so obviously lacking in the intimacy area that her overprotective aunt was trying to make sure she got some? A shudder ran through Ruth as she pressed the screen of her phone again in case a new message had popped up in the minute since she last looked. Something had probably come up with Ollie's father. Ruth could pop some popcorn and watch the movie she had rented with Piglet. She could use some alone time anyway, right?

The doorbell rang. Ruth stopped her pacing and stared at the door. Her plans for a solitary evening vanished as her racing heart picked up speed. At the light rapping on the wood, Ruth made her legs move toward the entrance and opened the door.

"Hey. I'm sorry I'm running late. I needed a shower and then I had to check Henry's meds and make sure they were set for the night and then...wow. You look beautiful."

Ollie glanced up mid-ramble and her eyes widened as Ruth's cheeks heated. Ruth hadn't been sure what kind of attire a second date taking place in her home required, so she had gone with one of her favourite summer dresses. The weather definitely didn't call for it yet, but they were indoors so she figured it would work.

"Thank you. I love this dress, it's super comfortable. Sorry, come in."

Ruth stepped back to let Ollie into the cottage. It was still relatively bright outside, but an evening breeze had a chill wrapping around her in the short time she held the door open.

"Hey there, beautiful girl."

Ruth shook her head and smiled at Ollie, who had been accosted by Piglet the moment Ruth's back was turned. Not that Ollie seemed to mind. Ruth took a moment to appreciate Ollie's attire while she was busy obeying Pig's request for belly scratches. Her casual shirt was open, revealing a tight string top clinging to her figure like it was a second skin. Ruth gulped as she moved her eyes lower, over the just-as-tight leggings moulding to Ollie in all the right places. Ruth's gaze stopped wandering once it reached Ollie's ass, a sight that would be burned into her mind forever more.

"Ahem," Ollie said.

Ruth startled and quickly moved her eyes up to meet Ollie's, which were sparkling in amusement. *Busted.* Ruth shrugged, deciding to go the confident route. Fake it till you make it and all that.

"You look good, too," Ruth said. She flicked her eyes back to Ollie's ass and up again, emphasising her point.

"So, what do you have planned for us?" Ollie met Ruth's gaze with a teasing grin.

Ruth walked toward her and tilted her head up to capture Ollie's lips in hers. It was a far quicker kiss than Ruth wanted, but she had plans for their date that required them to not be glued together immediately. As Ruth went to pull back, Ollie wrapped her arms around Ruth and pulled her in closer. She deepened the kiss with an obvious hunger. Suddenly, Ruth's plans seemed unimportant, and she got lost in the sensations of Ollie's tongue pressed against hers. Ruth let out a soft whimper as Ollie pulled back this time and placed a final soft kiss on Ruth's mouth.

"Not that I'm complaining, but is the date just kissing all night? If so, I'm definitely down for that. I just want to make sure I'm not derailing your grand plans that you wouldn't tell me about."

Ruth blinked a couple of times and tried to recall her plans, and her own name at that. Date, yes, that's what they were doing. Ollie watched her with an easy smile and eyes darkened with lust.

"Plans. Yes. Keep those lips over there, they are very distracting," Ruth said.

Ollie moved a tiny bit closer and whispered softly, "But

you're the one who kissed me first, darling. You can't blame me for being a distraction."

Ruth's body rippled with the desire that dripped from every word Ollie spoke. It took every ounce of willpower she had to step back and take Ollie's hand in hers, leading her toward the living room.

"Yes, yes, but your lips were asking to be kissed. So that's not my fault. But we have the whole evening ahead of us, so let's go."

They rounded the corner to the living room and Ollie immediately burst into laughter as Ruth held her hands out and said, "Voilà!"

Ruth had started the fire a little earlier, so the room was warm and comfortable. In front of the fire, she had set up a makeshift blanket fort, with blankets draped across the back of two chairs and an abundance of cushions inside to line the floor. Thank God for Greta's obsession with reading nooks and cushions. There were two trays set out with empty plates and packets of Tayto, and a Capri Sun next to each.

"The toasties are just in the sandwich maker, ready to be heated. Oh, and wait."

Ruth grabbed the remote and turned the TV off standby mode. The screen showed it was paused at the beginning of a cartoon movie.

"You can put on a different one if you want while I go grab the sandwiches," Ruth said.

Ruth was suddenly filled with nerves, worrying she had gone too far in her attempt to replicate their pretend ideal date. She wanted this to be an actual ideal date, too. Ollie grabbed her face and kissed her deeply before pressing her forehead to Ruth's. Her smile was wide and alleviated Ruth's fears.

"It's perfect. Now go get the sandwiches and meet me in the blanket fort."

Ruth was sure she had never heard a better sentence uttered in her life.

❖

"Favourite colour?"

"Blue," Olivia responded to Ruth's question on autopilot. She was distracted by the patterns Ruth's fingers were making up and down her arm. Ruth didn't even appear aware of the action, but Olivia's body certainly was.

"Okay, now what's your *real* favourite colour?" Ruth asked.

"My real favourite colour?" Olivia questioned.

"Yep. It's a standard get to know you question, and I bet that's your standard never changed since childhood answer. Am I wrong?"

"You're not wrong. It's not something I've spent a lot of time thinking about. I'll have to get back to you. What's yours?" Olivia asked.

"Today it's forest green." Ruth spoke the words while looking intently into Olivia's eyes.

"Does your favourite colour often change day by day?" Olivia asked. She realized as she looked into Ruth's blue eyes that her own childhood answer just might be accurate.

"Depends on what inspires it. Your eyes are usually sparkling, but the green is deeper tonight. Like a forest."

Olivia's mouth went dry and there was no doubt in her mind what was behind the deepening colour of her eyes. The same thing that drove the dampening between her legs and the goosebumps across every inch of her arm where Ruth's fingers grazed her skin.

"I never thought being seduced in a blanket fort would be on my top list of turn-ons," Olivia whispered.

"Who said anything about seducing? I was asking an innocent question." Ruth batted her eyelids for effect.

"I have a feeling you know exactly what you're doing, darling."

"I love when you call me that." Ruth's voice matched Olivia's whisper as the air around them grew thicker. The heat from their stares rivalled the heat from the smouldering fire.

"Is this the part of the date where we can kiss again? I loved the movie, and the sandwich dinner was surprisingly good, but I'm not sure I can wait much longer for the kissing part."

Olivia moved forward and paused for a moment to look at Ruth. Yep, blue was definitely her favourite colour, no doubt about it. She captured Ruth's lips in hers and she was sure at that moment she would never grow tired of this. Olivia warred between the part of her that longed to explore each and every inch of Ruth's body, and the part that wanted to spend forever kissing Ruth. Ruth had no such dilemma as she nudged Olivia back against the cushions and moved to cover Olivia's body with her own.

Ruth's traced her lips from Olivia's mouth across her jawline and down to her neck. Olivia groaned and reached around to pull Ruth closer, desperate for any friction. Her hands landed on bare thighs with just the hint of the material from Ruth's dress grazing her thumbs. She wanted Ruth so badly she could hardly comprehend all of the feelings swimming around her body.

Ruth pulled back and Olivia gasped at the loss of contact. She opened her eyes to find Ruth staring at her with flushed cheeks and wide eyes.

"Is this okay? Too fast?" Ruth's voice was huskier than usual when she spoke, and Olivia loved it.

"God no. I mean yes it's okay, no to the too-fast part."

Olivia stroked her fingers beneath the hem of Ruth's dress where it lay not far below Ruth's ass. Ruth's breath hitched and her eyes darkened at the action.

"Is it okay for you?" Olivia asked.

Ruth nodded and moved her hand up to stroke Olivia's cheek in a gesture that made Olivia's heart stop beating for a moment. They had done nothing but kiss really, and yet it was one of the most intimate experiences of Olivia's life.

"Do you want to move to my room? Greta's not coming home tonight, but I do have a bed we can continue this in."

The thought of Ruth's body leaving hers wasn't one that sat well with Olivia, so she shook her head slowly.

"Unless you have any objections, I'm good here. Wouldn't want to waste a perfectly good blanket fort."

Ruth's smile turned into a moan as Olivia moved her hands up beneath Ruth's dress and cupped her ass cheeks as she pulled Ruth closer against her.

"Fuck, I could get lost in you," Olivia said as Ruth leaned forward again, barely brushing her lips against Olivia's.

"So, what's stopping you?" Ruth spoke the words between soft kisses, and nothing in the world could've stopped Olivia then. She switched their positions, moving Ruth beneath her as she pressed her leg between Ruth's. Her thigh met Ruth's damp underwear as she captured her lips again and pressed more firmly against Ruth's heated centre.

"More, Ollie, please." Ruth pulled her head back and panted out the words as Olivia moved her thigh in a firm rhythm.

"Patience, darling." Olivia showed far more restraint than she expected as she stared into Ruth's eyes while keeping up the teasing her thigh was doing. She was going to give Ruth more, that was for certain. But right now, Olivia couldn't pull her eyes away from Ruth's beautiful face, filled with so much desperation. As Ruth's whimpers increased, Olivia replaced her thigh with her hand. She slid Ruth's soaked panties to the side and pressed a finger inside Ruth as she moved her thumb to stroke Ruth's clit.

Ruth gripped Olivia's shoulders. She dug her nails in lightly as Olivia added a second finger and picked up the pace of her motions while increasing pressure on Ruth's most sensitive spot. Ruth's hips bucked and increased Olivia's pace as all thoughts of taking things slowly fled from Olivia's mind. She moved faster and harder until Ruth's thighs squeezed together, halting her motions. Ruth clenched around Olivia's fingers and threw her head back as she came.

"Fuck, Olivia." Ruth's voice broke around the words and Olivia damn near growled at the sound. It was the first time Ruth had called her by her full name. As she heard it leave Ruth's lips mid-orgasm, she was sure her name had never sounded so good. Olivia stroked Ruth's cheek gently with her other hand still firmly between Ruth's legs. As her thighs relaxed, Ruth blinked her eyes open, and a soft smile graced her face. She gazed at Olivia with a look of pure bliss.

"We're still fully clothed," Ruth mumbled, and Olivia laughed.

"Yes, yes, we are. We should rectify that," Olivia said.

Ruth's smile broadened as she nodded and pushed Olivia back to pull at her shirt. Ruth was clearly on a mission to rectify it immediately, however that mission was swiftly interrupted as Olivia sat back to give Ruth more room to manoeuvre. In the process of doing so, Olivia knocked the blankets off their precarious position atop the chair and they found themselves buried beneath a heavy pile of those blankets. Olivia wasn't sure which of them started laughing first, but soon the blankets were moving from the laughter shaking their bodies beneath.

"I think we broke the blanket fort," Ruth whispered, as Olivia managed to push the covers down enough to let their heads escape for air.

"Worth it," Olivia replied before she lost herself in Ruth's lips once more.

CHAPTER NINE

I need water so bad but I'm pretty sure my legs have stopped working."

Ruth turned her head at Ollie's words and chuckled. They had found their way to Ruth's bed not long ago and continued their thorough exploration of each other's bodies. Her own mouth was dry from exertion, but her aching thighs didn't want to move.

"Same. I wish Piglet was trained to fetch drinks and stuff because I'm not sure I'll make it to the kitchen," Ruth said.

Ollie turned onto her side to face Ruth and ran one finger slowly up and down Ruth's abdomen. Ruth's skin prickled beneath the contact. Her body responded automatically to Ollie as she moved into the touch.

"What if I make it worth your while?"

Ollie's husky voice sent shivers through Ruth in all the right places. She had been sure just a moment ago that she had no energy left, yet suddenly her limbs were reenergized at the prospect of more of whatever Ollie had to offer. The offerings she had witnessed already were enough proof it was worth it.

"Depends on what you had in mind. It's a long walk on shaky legs, you know."

Ruth batted her eyelashes, all the while knowing she

would crawl if she had to. Ollie grinned and leaned in to place a soft kiss against the corner of Ruth's lips.

She moved her lips to Ruth's ear and whispered softly, "Well, once I'm hydrated again, I'm sure my mouth can find many ways to thank you for it."

Ollie sucked gently on Ruth's earlobe as Ruth's stomach did somersaults. She clenched her thighs together as the throbbing picked up pace between her legs once more.

"Shit, Ollie. You're too good at this. You win."

Ruth hopped off the bed and made her way to the kitchen. Her legs thankfully stayed upright for the journey, despite their protesting aches. She took in the sight of their ruined blanket fort on the floor of the living room and smiled. They had put it to good use, that was for sure. Never had Ruth imagined that she would find someone who not only entertained her notion of a blanket fort date with sandwiches and cartoons, but genuinely enjoyed it. Ruth's anxiety, while always somewhere beneath the surface, had been quiet all evening. Ollie had been so vocal and reassuring about how much fun she was having that Ruth hadn't had a moment to consider otherwise. It was refreshing.

She returned to her room with two bottles of water held up like a treasured prize. The sight of Ollie lounging naked in her bed made her pause for a moment. Pulling out her phone to take a photo would likely be inappropriate, but she wanted to capture the moment as a snapshot in her head.

"I have returned from my mission. For you, madam."

Ruth hopped back onto the bed and held a bottle out to Ollie, who had it open and against her mouth in record time. Ollie gulped the water like it was the first liquid to pass her lips after being stuck in a desert. Somehow, even that sight had Ruth's body reacting.

"You gonna drink that, or just watch me?" Ollie asked.

Ruth flicked her gaze up and met Ollie's eyes as they sparkled with amusement. Ruth shrugged before leaning in to wipe a drop of water from the corner of Ollie's lips.

"Why not both?"

Ruth opened her own bottle and pulled it to her lips. She kept her eyes trained on Ollie as the cool liquid slid down her throat. The look in Ollie's eyes turned from one of amusement to one filled with lust. Ruth hadn't realized how erotic something as simple as drinking water could be. As her eyes stayed locked with Ollie's while she finished the water, the look shifted again. Ruth had been eager to hydrate and claim her reward, but what started as simple teasing had somehow turned far more intimate.

"Are you my girlfriend?" Ollie blurted.

Ruth choked on the last sip of water in her mouth and coughed. It was a simple question, so why did it have her heart racing and her mouth scrambling for words?

"Sorry. That was a silly way to approach this. It's just, we never really defined anything, and my sister was calling you my girlfriend earlier, and I liked it, so…"

Ruth smiled as a warmth grew in her chest at Ollie's babbling and reddened cheeks.

"You liked it, eh?" Ruth teased, as she placed her empty water bottle on the bedside locker beside Ollie's.

Her teasing smile slipped at the intensity of Ollie's expression when Ruth turned back to face her. She sat and crossed her legs to mirror Ollie's pose. She placed a hand over Ollie's where it rested on her knee. It struck Ruth how comfortable she was facing Ollie and having this conversation in her bed while totally naked.

"We should've probably discussed this before, you know…" Ollie darted her eyes to the side, a sheepish look on her face. She was nervous. That realisation brought a strange level of confidence to Ruth. The one salve for her anxiety had always been being the one to be able to ease someone else's.

"If we're grown up enough to do it, we're definitely grown up enough to discuss it. What's worrying you? I haven't been with anyone else in a long time, and I've been tested since." Ruth offered the information, wondering if Ollie was hesitant to ask for it. It was probably a discussion they should have had before sleeping together, as Ollie had said, but better late than never. Ruth stroked her thumb along Ollie's palm in what she hoped was a soothing motion.

"No, I didn't mean that. Thank you for telling me, though. And same here. My last relationship didn't end so well. I got tested right after I found out how many other people she had been sleeping with over the two years we were together, and I was thankfully all good. I only slept with one other person since then, not recently, and we were safe. But I'm happy to get tested again if you want."

Ruth squeezed Ollie's hand softly. "I'm sorry about your ex. That really sucks."

"It did. I moved to the city after that, trying to put distance between us. I knew given the chance, she would try to worm her way back into my life, and I didn't know if I was strong enough to resist. So, when the job opened up in the city hospital, I just packed and left. My best friend lives there so I crashed with her for a while. I changed my number, blocked her on all social media, and basically disappeared."

Ruth had known that Ollie moved to the city not long before her, but she hadn't realized Ollie had been running from something. Or someone, it seemed.

"Wow, I can't imagine doing that. I've had the same number since I first got a phone, and well, everyone I'm close to lives in this village. Disappearing from one person would mean disappearing from everyone, really."

Ollie nodded, and a soft sadness clouded her features.

"Yeah, I basically lost all my friends when we broke up. I realized when things were falling apart that I had created my life there around her. All my friends were really her friends, the place we lived was her apartment that I moved into. All the furniture was hers, even my job was in her family's medical practice. I had slotted right into her life, and I slotted right out, leaving her with everything she had always had and me with, well, nothing."

Ruth didn't know what to say, or more likely if what she wanted to say was appropriate.

"She didn't have everything," Ruth said. Ollie glanced up as Ruth continued. "She doesn't have you. Seems like a big loss to me."

Ollie smiled and reached out to stroke Ruth's cheek gently.

"Sorry for pulling down the mood," Ollie said.

Ruth pressed a finger to Ollie's lips and shook her head.

"No, don't go there. I want to know everything, Ollie. The good and bad, and everything in between."

Ollie's eyes softened and she pressed a gentle kiss to Ruth's finger where it still lay against her lips.

"So, what did you mean? When you started you said we should have discussed it before...but then you said it wasn't about being tested. So, what did you mean?" Ruth asked.

"Well, it's just...I guess...what we are. Things can get messy if people aren't on the same page. There were so many red flags at the start of my last relationship, but she used the fact that we never defined ourselves as anything to convince me I was overreacting. And I still stayed, until two years later the same red flags were still there. I felt so ridiculous that I let her treat me that way, it's not like there were no signs."

Ruth shook her head vehemently. "No, don't do that. You didn't let her do anything. It sounds to me like she did what she wanted, and then she manipulated you into blaming yourself. She gets that blame, not you, understand?"

Ollie looked a little taken aback by the force in Ruth's words, but she nodded.

"The thing is, my life was in a far less messy place back then than it is right now. I'm worried that jumping into something while I'm dealing with everything with Henry and all that brings isn't the smartest move."

Ruth's heart began to sink, and her confidence slowly faded with each word. She caught herself before her thoughts jumped to the worst possible conclusions. Ollie wouldn't be sitting there in her bed saying any of this unless she thought it was beneficial to them both. Ruth had to trust that.

"But you have been the one shining bright spot to everything for me, and it definitely doesn't seem smart to ignore that. I don't know what the next few weeks will bring for me, but I do know that I want you. I just want to be sure we're on the same page," Ollie said.

Ruth cradled Ollie's face in her hands and stared into the beautiful eyes filled with sad memories and hope.

"I want you, too, Ollie. And despite what ending up in bed together on our second date may look like, we're not jumping into anything. If you total the amount of talking we've done daily for the past almost two months, it probably tallies up to a year or so of weekly dates."

Ollie laughed and Ruth couldn't help herself from leaning in to sneak another kiss. She meant it to be a quick one, but when Ollie's arms pulled her closer, she couldn't pull away. The kiss deepened, along with the feelings bubbling up inside Ruth.

"Yes."

Ruth whispered the one simple word against Ollie's lips

between kisses. Ollie pulled back and looked into Ruth's eyes, as if they held the meaning of Ruth's answer.

"Yes, I'm your girlfriend. And yes, that can mean a lot of different things to a lot of different people, so we can discuss our definition. But what I can assure you is it means the only person I do any of this with is you," Ruth said.

Ollie pushed Ruth onto her back and hovered above her with the widest smile on her face.

"Yes, we can discuss it later. Because right now, I believe you were owed a reward, darling. Although—" Ollie paused as she ran her eyes up and down Ruth's body slowly and deliberately. She knelt between Ruth's open legs and licked her lips in a way that made Ruth's breath catch before continuing, "I'm pretty sure I'm the one being rewarded."

❖

"You're happier today."

Olivia glanced up at Henry from where she stood washing the dishes that didn't fit in the dishwasher. People had taken to dropping off homemade meals every few days now, which had been a life saver in terms of saving her time with cooking. However, keeping track of who owned which dish was becoming a problem.

"Are you okay?" Olivia set the pan down and dried her hands on a towel before she moved toward him.

"I'm fine, I can sit by myself."

Henry took a seat at the table and Olivia hovered, unsure what to do. Should she join him, or go back to what she had been doing? He kicked out a chair and nodded, indicating for her to sit. The teenage rebellious side of her baulked at the idea, and she almost turned on her heel and walked back to the sink. Her mind flashed back to Grace's worried face when she had asked Olivia if she talked to him while Grace wasn't around. Olivia sighed and took a seat as she looked into her father's eyes.

"You were whistling."

Henry smiled softly, which was the first smile she had seen from him in days. He looked even thinner and paler than he had when Olivia arrived, which seemed like a lifetime ago already.

"I don't whistle," Olivia grumbled.

A small laugh escaped his lips, and he shook his head slowly. "Still as stubborn as ever. Must've been imagining those sweet tunes that drew me down here, then," Henry said.

He whistled softly, mimicking the tune Olivia always unconsciously broke into whenever she was deep in happy memories. It was a lifelong habit and a clear indicator of her mood for anyone who was around long enough to pick up on the pattern.

"Okay, maybe I was whistling a little bit. It's a habit," Olivia said.

Henry nodded. "I know. You started copying me when you were little. I used to whistle around the house. I'd hear a tiny little whistle in reply, and I'd find you giggling somewhere waiting for me to find you."

His nostalgic smile grated on Olivia, and she suppressed the urge to get up and walk away. She couldn't suppress the words that slipped out, though.

"I spent a long time waiting for you."

Henry nodded again and his smile dimmed a little but didn't quite disappear.

"You did, Livvie. Now tell me, who's got you whistling this time?"

Henry's quick acceptance of her anger, without meeting it with defence or even excuses, surprised her.

"Who says it's a who? Can't a woman just be happy alone?" Olivia frowned, unsure how much Henry already knew. Especially considering Mrs Guiney had been yapping in his ear the night before. Damn the small village gossip mill.

"I'm sure she can. But your sister has never been very good at keeping things to herself. She tells me you've been seeing Ruth Miller. Is she the one who's got you looking so sappy?"

At the mention of Ruth's name, Olivia smiled. She quickly changed to a neutral expression at the knowing nod from Henry.

"She's a good one, Ruth. She's not had the easiest time of it, but she always has time for anyone who needs it. I thought she'd have called 'round when she got back."

A slight frown appeared between Henry's eyes.

"She usually stopped by for a chat. I guess she knows…"

He trailed off, and Olivia filled in the blanks for him.

"You think I've turned her against you out of spite? I didn't even know she lived here until I ran into her down in the village. We met online."

Henry shook his head quickly. "No, no. I don't think you'd do anything of the sort. However she feels about me after hearing the truth, you didn't do anything wrong. Plus, if she keeps making you smile like you did today, that's worth it."

A mix of emotions washed through Olivia. It was too much—it was all too much. She didn't need Henry's approval, and yet some part of her still brightened at his easy acceptance of her and Ruth.

"Ruth mentioned wanting to visit when I first got here.

You've just been sleeping a lot, and I didn't know if you'd be up for it." *Or if I would.*

Henry's face brightened. "Tell her to come around when she has a chance. You two can hang out here. Make her some dinner or something, eh? I probably won't be up for chatting too long. Speaking of which, I'm wiped now."

Olivia nodded and helped him out of the chair. She made sure he got back to the room safely. He was out like a light the minute his head hit the pillow, and Olivia spent a moment adjusting his blankets to make sure he was comfortable. She pulled out her phone to text Ruth and invite her around the following evening. Olivia didn't want to be the one to get in the way of anyone's chance to spend time with Henry, regardless of her own feelings around him. Especially when there likely wasn't long left to spend.

CHAPTER TEN

Ruth knocked on the door and waited nervously for Ollie to answer. She had been to Mr B.'s house a few times over the past year, ever since Mr B.'s health declined enough that he stopped working. Ruth always came with a box of chocolates as a nod to the chocolates he used to leave for her all those years ago. She gripped the box tight in her hand and wondered if she should knock again.

Before Ruth could make up her mind, the door opened to reveal a dishevelled looking Ollie.

"Sorry, I was trying to make dinner, and then Henry fell, and the place is a mess and I—"

"Mr B. fell? Is he okay?"

Ruth let herself in, closing the door behind her and following Ollie into the kitchen. Ruth glanced around as Ollie scraped what looked like the remnants of a charred curry into the bin. Ollie was right, the place *was* a mess. It would be endearing to see Ollie so ruffled, if it wasn't for her concern about the fall.

"Yeah, he's fine. He got up to go to the bathroom and naturally decided to leave his walker behind and not ask for help."

Frustration was evident in Ollie's tone. Ruth placed a

hand on the back of Ollie's neck and Ollie sighed, leaning into the touch.

"He's okay. I just got a fright when I heard the thump. I was on track with everything, and I would've had plenty of time to clean up the mess, but I ran in to check and forgot all about the dinner. He was already getting back up when I got there. I got him settled again and checked him over, and apart from embarrassment, he was fine. By the time I got back down here our chicken curry, however, was not."

Ollie placed the pot on the countertop next to the rest of the items used for meal prep. She turned, and Ruth saw her eyes brimming with unshed tears mixed with a hint of exhaustion.

"I'm sorry," Ollie whispered.

Ruth pulled Ollie close, enveloping her in a tight hug. "If you've got cheese and bread, I make a mean toastie."

Ollie's body shook in Ruth's arms as she laughed but didn't let go. "We can't have that for every date."

Ruth pulled back slightly and donned her best serious face. "Don't ruin a good thing."

Ollie's eyes dropped to Ruth's lips, and she leaned in to kiss her softly. "You're good at making me feel a little less of a mess." Ollie spoke the words against Ruth's lips and kissed her more.

"Oh, you're definitely a mess. But you're my mess." Ruth said the words lightly, hoping to keep Ollie's smile in place. She wasn't prepared for the soft look that Ollie gave her at the words.

"Yours," Ollie whispered.

The inflection in the word added a whole layer to the meaning, and Ruth almost looked away from the intensity of the moment. She had no idea how they'd wound up here so soon, but the undeniable depth of their feelings hung between them.

"You could've at least tidied up for the girl."

Mr B.'s teasing tone cut between them, and Ruth smiled at him as he walked into the room. He was thankfully using the walker this time.

"I would have if you had used your walker, Henry. What are you doing out of bed?"

Henry. Of course, Ruth knew Mr B.'s name, but hearing it come from Ollie was a surprise. Despite their strained relationship she'd still expected that Ollie would call him Dad.

"I heard the door and I wanted to come say hi. Which is easier to do now since you made me move rooms. Maybe you should let me get back to my own room and then you'd hear me coming down the stairlift, so you'd have time to stop making googly eyes at each other."

A hint of a smile graced Ollie's lips before she extinguished it with a shake of her head. "No, then I'd likely be dealing with you falling down the stairs instead of just on the carpeted floor. The bedroom down here is just as good as yours, I even had your bed moved."

Ruth watched the back and forth between father and daughter, the resemblance that she had missed before now uncanny. Not that she would say so to Ollie anytime soon.

"Ruth, my dear. It's good to see you."

Mr B. made his way toward her slowly, and Ruth's heart panged with sadness. The once strong, lively man now looked weak and frail. Much more so than the last time she'd seen him, which had been only a few months prior.

"Hey, Mr B. It's good to see you, too."

Ruth gave him a quick hug and handed him the box of chocolates she had placed on the table.

"My favourite."

Mr B. grinned as he opened the box, and as always, he handed her the chocolate wrapped in golden foil. Ruth smiled at the familiar ritual as she placed the chocolate into her pocket for later. Ollie stood off to the side and watched the scene with a guarded expression. As Ruth stood there in front of Mr B. again, it was so hard for her to connect the man before her with the man that had hurt Ollie so badly.

"Anyway, I just wanted to say a quick hello. I need to head back to bed now, before I give this one another heart attack."

He whispered the last sentence and winked. It was loud enough to make Ollie roll her eyes as Ruth grinned. They both watched him turn to walk back. He was noticeably even slower than his walk in. Ollie had a look of concern on her face, one that held far more emotion than Ollie would likely admit. When Mr B. got out of earshot, Ruth walked toward Ollie and lowered her voice, not wanting to offend him.

"You go make sure he's okay and I'll tidy up here. Take your time."

Ollie nodded, but the look of concern on her face was unwavering.

"He's due his meds anyway, so it might be a few minutes. I can tidy when I get back, though. The living room is pretty clear if you want to go sit."

Ruth kissed Ollie's cheek and pushed her toward the hallway Mr B. had gone down.

"Go. I'm fine."

Ollie quickly followed her father as Ruth set about clearing up the mess before her. She made quick work of it, placing most of the ware in the dishwasher and stacking what remained neatly by the sink.

"Wow. How'd you work this magic so quickly?"

Ruth jumped as Ollie came up behind her, wrapping her arms around Ruth's waist.

"Believe it or not, I like cleaning. And organising. Anything to keep me busy and out of my head. It calms me."

Ruth turned in Ollie's arms and wrapped hers around Ollie's shoulders.

"I suck at anything to do with cleaning, so I am very grateful for the weird way you calm yourself."

Ruth grinned and kissed Ollie softly as she pulled her closer. She loved the feeling of Ollie's body pressed tight against hers.

"One of the ways. I'm definitely discovering more."

❖

Olivia's phone buzzed on the bedside locker as she rolled over in her bed and out of Ruth's arms. She grabbed the phone before the vibration woke Ruth and glanced at the screen, closing her eyes briefly. She walked to her ensuite bathroom and shut the door behind her before clicking answer on the call.

"Hi, Mom."

"Oh, so you're alive, then?"

The words could be taken teasingly, however the tone certainly couldn't. Olivia sat on the edge of the bathtub and braced herself for what she knew was coming.

"I texted you last week."

"Oh, thanks for taking the effort to send me one sentence, Livvie. Clearly your *father* gets your attention these days."

The way her mother spat out the word father had Olivia's gut clenching.

"He's dying, Mom. We're not having a happy family reunion. You know how it's been for Grace. I'm here for her."

At the mention of her sister's name, her mother sighed and changed her tone.

"Yes, it's hard for Gracie. I'm glad she's got you taking care of her."

When have I ever not, Olivia thought. Most of her conversations with her mother took place inside her head these days.

"I was talking to Grace yesterday and she mentioned she has a few days off college next week. I had asked her to call to see me, but she's intent on spending it with Henry. So, while she's there, you can come instead."

The words that were spoken so casually had Olivia gripping the edge of the tub so tightly that her knuckles whitened from the pressure. The funny thing was, there was no malice behind it. Her mom didn't see the problem with mentioning that Olivia was her second pick to spend time with, or with her assumption that Olivia would have nothing better to do with her time at such short notice.

"There's still a lot to be done here. Henry isn't doing well, and I don't want to be gone for long while things are…"

Olivia trailed off, not knowing exactly how to say it. *While he's so close to dying? While I'm dangling on the edge of maybe finding some semblance of closure before that happens?* Neither sentence would go down well with her mom, so she stopped speaking altogether.

"Your sister will be there. I'm sure he doesn't need you both hovering over him, he managed quite well without you for long enough. And from the way your sister describes it, he's practically a celebrity in that little village he fled to. I need to see you, Livvie, it's important."

Olivia frowned at the change in her mom's tone. "What's wrong? What happened?"

Silence greeted her on the other end, until finally her mother spoke again. "Nothing as important as dying, don't worry. I need to go now, but I'll see you next week and we can catch up properly."

The line cut off before Olivia had a chance to get any further information, or even say goodbye. She sat for another moment, head spinning with all the potential things her mom could be summoning her for. The options were wide and varied. One time, her mom had deemed it urgent to get Olivia to fix her new Wi-Fi router. Apparently, she had been unable to read the instructions herself. Another time, she had a suspicious mole on her back that she only trusted her daughter the nurse to look at, as if she didn't have a whole clinic up the road who were far more capable at doing so. The time before that it was to deal with a scam her mom had fallen for that involved giving her bank details via email. Big or small, her mom called, and Olivia answered. Her mom needed something, and Olivia took care of it.

There could be weeks, months, sometimes even a year between the urgent requests. But inevitably, it would come. Most of the time, it conveniently happened when her mom knew Olivia was needed elsewhere. Time and time again Olivia told herself she wouldn't drop everything and run when her mother clicked her fingers. Next time she would ask for, no, demand more information first. Next time she would say no. Next time never came, though, and now here Olivia was, a grown woman sitting on the edge of her bathtub setting boundaries with her mother in her head that she would never uphold in real life.

A soft knock came on the door and Olivia remembered she wasn't alone in her bedroom. *Ruth.* She walked to the door and opened it, noting the concern etched into Ruth's features.

"Are you okay?"

Ruth's voice was shaky, and she was fidgeting with her hands as she waited for Olivia's reply. Ruth's eyes weren't meeting Olivia's, and Olivia noticed she had a long T-shirt on. Olivia's T-shirt. Olivia wasn't sure exactly how long she'd been in the bathroom, or how long Ruth had been waiting awake in her bed wondering where Olivia was.

"Sorry, yes. I just got a call from my mom that I had to take. I didn't mean to take so long."

Olivia reached out to grip one of Ruth's hands in hers and hoped it would provide some reassurance that Olivia's absence when she woke wasn't about her. Ruth nodded, but her clammy hand still shook in Olivia's. Olivia led her to the bed and sat down, lifting Ruth's chin softly.

"Hey, it's okay. I'm here." Olivia spoke in soft whispers as Ruth's features relaxed a tiny bit. She was taking slow, deep breaths in and out, and Olivia noticed that the fidgeting was a pattern, her thumb touching each finger in repetition.

"Are you okay?" Olivia asked.

Ruth nodded but stayed quiet for a few more moments until the fidgeting stopped. Eventually, she nodded more firmly.

"I'm sorry. I woke and waited, and when you didn't return, I got worried."

Ruth shrugged and her cheeks turned pink as she continued.

"My mind went to a lot of places that really don't make much sense, but I started to panic, and I didn't know what to do. It's silly, I know. But sometimes I can't always help it. Especially when I'm in unfamiliar places."

Olivia ran her hand up and down Ruth's arm.

"It's not silly. I'm glad you knocked. The patterns you were doing, that helps?" Olivia nodded toward Ruth's fingers.

"Yes. It's something I've done since I was a kid. Patterns have always grounded me. I used to try to stop it, so I didn't look weird, but part of my therapy was realising I was doing it to help myself and that's a good thing. I have a few techniques

I use to calm myself when my anxiety starts building, but that's generally my go to."

Olivia smiled and pulled Ruth's fingers up to her lips to kiss them softly.

"It's smart. You'll always have them on hand, pun intended. I'd like to know about what helps, or maybe signs for me to look out for."

Ruth raised her eyes to Olivia's and looked at her fully for the first time since Olivia left the bathroom.

"You would?"

The soft, hopeful tone made Ruth sound vulnerable. It filled Olivia with a deep sense of wanting to protect her from anything that could fill her with this worry.

"Of course. I know I can't fix it, or make it go away. But if there's ways I can help you move through it, or things I can do to make it a little easier, I want to."

Ruth placed a kiss on Olivia's lips and whispered a soft thank you. They sat together a little longer as the shaking in Ruth's hands stopped completely and her breathing became more natural than forced.

"Is your mom okay? You looked a little angry when you opened the door," Ruth asked.

Olivia had been so focused on Ruth that she had already forgotten all about the conversation with her mom.

"She wants me to visit next week, when Grace is down with Henry. She said she needs to talk to me about something."

"You must be worried. It must be important for her to bother you while you're dealing with everything here," Ruth said.

"You'd think so," Olivia scoffed, and Ruth looked at her in confusion. Of course, without any context, the words would sound harsh to anyone.

"My mom has a habit of urgently needing me anytime she

knows I'm giving someone else my time and attention. It's always been this way."

Ruth nodded. The confusion was still present, but she held Olivia's hand tighter in hers.

"I'm sorry. That sounds tough. Are you going to go?"

Olivia shrugged, but the answer was yes. The fallout of not going would be harder to deal with right now than giving her mom what she wanted.

"Hey, you said you wanted to find out more about your parents and where you grew up, right? Why don't you come with me? At least then there would be a purpose to the trip other than succumbing to my mom's whims."

Ruth looked hesitant, and Olivia winced.

"I'm sorry. That was insensitive. Learning about your parents is a big deal, and I shouldn't have made it an afterthought. I had just been hoping to spend that time with you, when Grace was here, but I understand if it's too much, too soon."

Ruth thought about it for a moment. A range of emotions flitted across her face as Olivia gave her the time to process.

"Let's do it. I'm not sure how ready I'll be to delve into the stuff about my parents, but a trip with you sounds good either way. It's not like I have to go looking if I change my mind."

Olivia wrapped her arms around Ruth and hugged her close. Suddenly, the thought of travelling home to her mom sounded far less daunting with Ruth at her side.

CHAPTER ELEVEN

I made a road trip playlist."

Ruth closed the door of the boot and slid into the passenger seat of Ollie's car.

"You and your lists," Ollie grumbled with a small smile before brushing her lips against Ruth's. It was definitely the best way to say hello.

"It's a playlist. That's different to a regular list. However, I have one of those, too."

Ollie shook her head in amusement as her smile widened.

"What could you possibly have a list for?"

Ruth pulled out her phone and opened her notes app, the keeper of all her lists, ideas, and random musings.

"Well, I made a list of all the possible places I could go to find out more about my parents if I still want to while we're there. Just some things I remember from the little tidbits my aunt has said throughout the years, and some stuff I have from a memory box. Most of my things were lost in the fire, but my aunt salvaged what she could and kept it in a box for me until I was ready to look."

"A fire, that's what happened?" Ollie asked tentatively.

It occurred to Ruth then that she had never told Ollie how her parents died, only that it had happened.

"Yeah, that's how they died. Our house caught fire—something about a frying pan in the kitchen. I don't remember much, just bits and pieces after I woke up in the hospital. The fireman that saved me died in the fire, too. I read an article about it once I was old enough to know how to google, but I stopped after the first. The details didn't make the outcome any easier."

Ollie was silent for a moment as she navigated the car along the winding dirt roads toward the dual carriageway that would bring them most of the way there.

"I'm sorry. I knew you lost your parents, but I didn't know you lost everything. Do you have photos or anything?"

Ruth shook her head softly, which was a gesture she realized Ollie couldn't see with her eyes on the road ahead.

"Not really. I have one photo of their wedding that survived with a layer of soot. Greta got it professionally cleaned and redone as best as possible. That's about it."

Ollie reached her hand across and squeezed Ruth's gently, before putting it back on the gear stick.

"We can take this at your pace. As much or as little as you want to explore, I'll be here. Well, assuming we survive my mother first." Ollie's laugh was hollow, and Ruth noted how different it was to Ollie's real laugh. The one that made Ruth's heart fill from the sound.

"Moms like me. Don't worry. I'm charming." Ruth exaggerated the last word and Ollie grinned.

"And modest, too, don't forget," Ollie said.

The rest of the journey passed quicker than Ruth would've liked. They talked about past relationships and Ollie gave more detail about her ex. Details that made Ruth, who never resorted to violence, want to punch the faceless woman. Ruth gave Ollie a brief history of her short and rather dull love life, up until now that was. They sang along to the music in between conversations and enjoyed each other's company. It was something Ruth realized was an underrated activity. Existing beside another person and enjoying the feeling of being with them was now highest on her list of daily joys.

As they drew nearer to their destination, Ollie chewed her lip so much Ruth worried it would start to bleed. That was usually Ruth's bad habit, something that signalled her own heightened anxiety.

"It's going to be okay," Ruth said, even though they both knew she had no information to make that claim with.

Ollie nodded but continued to gnaw on her bottom lip with her eyes straight ahead. Ruth grabbed her phone and clicked through the songs until she found a classic, one she was sure nobody could resist singing. As the notes to "I Will Survive" filled the car, her assumption proved correct as Ollie's lip found its release from between her teeth and the first words of the song left her mouth. Within seconds, they were both belting out the lyrics as if they'd been a duo for years, slipping into their respective roles in the tune seamlessly.

As the melody came to an end, Ollie was grinning despite their destination coming into view ahead of them. Music was magical, as was Ollie's infectious smile. Ollie pulled the car in to park on the street in front of a two-storey house in a row of almost identical houses.

"Home sweet home," Ollie muttered, shutting off the engine but making no move to exit the vehicle. Ruth stayed where she was, as determined to take this part at Ollie's pace as Ollie was to take the rest of their trip at Ruth's. The only move Ruth made was to slide her hand across the gap between their seats and onto Ollie's shaking arm, squeezing softly. Ollie locked their fingers together as she adjusted her gaze from the house before them to Ruth's face.

"You ready?" Ollie asked softly.

"Are you?" Ruth replied. That was the far more important part. Ollie shrugged, but after a sigh she unbuckled her seatbelt, and they made their way out of the car and toward the generic white front door. Ollie gave a brief knock and walked in with Ruth at her heels. She wanted to be close enough to give whatever support Ollie needed.

"I'm in here, Livvie."

Livvie. The name scratched at Ruth's brain, and she wondered why it was so familiar. She must've heard Mr B. referencing Livvie before she knew Livvie was her Ollie. *Her Ollie.* The thought made Ruth want to pinch herself to make sure it was all real. As they walked through the door to what seemed to be a living room turned craft room, Ollie's mother stood to pull Ollie into a tight hug.

"I missed you, baby."

"Missed you, too, Mom," Ollie said, and the words at least sounded sincere to Ruth. She watched the embrace with interest. Ruth didn't have much first-hand experience with the mother-daughter dynamics she'd read so much about, but it was clear Ollie wasn't an unwilling participant in the exchange.

Although Greta had been her guardian and parent since she was six, they had never had a standard mother-daughter relationship, or at least any that Ruth had stereotypically seen. Greta had always been her aunt, and although she was firm with Ruth, it had rarely been needed. Ruth hadn't been one to defy the rules often or engage in a battle of wills with Greta. Ruth had had a lot of freedom to explore and grow in her own way within the village of Wicker Hill.

So much so that Ruth hadn't realized how protected or guarded she actually was until she stepped outside of the comfort of the village and left for the city, which had been a short-lived, anxiety-filled adventure. Ruth hadn't appreciated or even noticed how much Greta did to manage Ruth's anxiety at home. Those were things Ruth struggled to do when she found herself alone. Back in the comforts of Wicker Hill, her anxiety was more at bay again, even if her worries about wasting her life were not.

Ruth was shaken from her thoughts as Ollie turned to introduce them both.

"Mom, this is my girlfriend, Ruth. Ruth, my mom."

Ruth waved awkwardly, never quite knowing the right greeting to give in situations that didn't formally require a handshake or naturally lead to a hug. Ollie's mom had no such qualms as she reached in to pull Ruth into a thankfully quicker embrace than Ollie had gotten.

"Call me Ellen, dear. It's great to meet you, even if it's the first I'm hearing about you."

Ellen shot Ollie a stern look, and Ollie's face turned a bright shade of red.

"I was going to tell you," Ollie mumbled, averting her eyes. Ellen beamed a smile back at Ruth and rolled her eyes playfully.

"Mind my daughter's manners, Ruth. She's never been good at sharing. I'll get all the details from you later." Ellen winked at Ruth conspiratorially. Ollie looked uncomfortable at the idea, and Ruth had a niggling feeling that there were some undertones to Ellen's words that Ruth was missing.

"Do you want to talk now, Mom?" Ollie asked.

"I can grab our bags from the car and let you two—"

Ruth was cut off mid-sentence as Ellen shook her head and practically shooed Ollie away.

"Nonsense, you just got here. Livvie can go grab the bags while we get acquainted. I have food out for lunch, so meet us at the table once you're done, Livvie."

Ruth glanced back at Ollie, whose face had turned from nerves to frustration as Ellen led Ruth through a set of double doors that opened into the kitchen. The small dining room table was set for three with a spread of breads, meats, and cheeses all set out. Ruth slid into a seat as Ellen took the one across from her.

"So, are you the reason my daughter is still stuck in that little village?"

❖

Olivia walked back into the house and dropped the bags near the entrance. Leaving Ruth alone with her mom for too long wasn't a smart idea, something that was confirmed when she walked into the kitchen and saw Ruth's uncomfortable smile as she appeared to grapple for words.

"I wouldn't quite say that. There's a shop and post office and café and stuff, but the nearest town is only about twenty minutes away, so it's not exactly isolated."

Olivia joined them at the table and hoped the parts of the conversation that she missed hadn't been too invasive.

"No interrogations please, Mom," Olivia pleaded.

It was a likely fruitless request, but she had to try.

"Oh hush, don't be dramatic. I was asking Ruth here about that lovely little village. I have to get my information from somewhere when you don't tell me anything."

Olivia groaned inward and hoped her face didn't convey her annoyance because that would only make things worse. Her mom was an expert at passive aggressive, and Olivia had learned not to rise to it. Well, mostly learned—she was only human, after all.

"You wanted to talk to me. What's going on?" Olivia wanted to get this part of the trip out of the way and deal with whatever crisis of the month her mom needed help with so she could focus on helping Ruth. Her mom however wasn't playing ball.

"We can talk about all that later, I'm trying to get to know your girlfriend. So, Ruth, have you always lived in this village? It must've been hard growing up without many other kids around. Do your parents run a farm or something?"

"A farm?" Ruth's attempts to keep up with Ellen's line of questioning had Olivia regretting not warning her more on their trip here. One thing about her mom was every question was either a statement in disguise or a building block to the real information she was looking for.

"Did Ruth tell you she's a photographer? Her work is great," Olivia said.

Olivia hoped by providing her mom with information about Ruth she would allow the change of topic without too much fuss. Olivia had learned her own tricks over the years, even if she wasn't always proud of her ability to manipulate a conversation almost as well as her mother. Olivia didn't however derive the same pleasure from it that her mom did.

"That's interesting. Is it like scenic photos?"

Her mom kept the same smile on her face as she played the role of clueless, curious city woman to a T. Olivia wasn't sure exactly where this was going, but she was certain it was going somewhere she wouldn't like.

"My work is a bit of a mixture. I do some event work. I have a wedding coming up in the city in a couple of weeks actually. I've also had some photos in exhibitions, and I sell some prints online, too," Ruth replied.

"Your parents must be very proud. Are you going to move to the city then, when Livvie comes back soon? I imagine there would be far more opportunities available to you there, especially the likes of events."

Olivia gritted her teeth and silently cursed her mother for dumping them into a topic they had yet to venture on themselves.

"I did live in the city for a while, but I recently moved back to Wicker Hill. I live with my aunt. The people in the village are very good at local support, and word of mouth goes a long way, too. They may be a small bunch, but their reach is pretty far. Between that and the contacts I made in the city, I'm kept busy."

Ruth's smile was genuine and her pride in her community was evident. A community that Olivia found herself strangely protective of, too. Considering not too long ago she wanted nothing to do with the place where Henry had made a home and discovered a new, albeit unconventional, family.

"That's nice that they look out for you, and that your aunt lets you live with her while you're figuring things out. You're still young, no rush with settling down. I'm glad these days there's not so much pressure to jump into marriage and babies and all of that when you're barely out of school. Look where that got me."

Her mom chuckled at the end, as if the notes of laughter would soften the sting of the words. Olivia's face must've held a hint of the hurt she tried so hard to hide because her mom reached out and took her hand while simultaneously rolling her eyes.

"Oh, you know I'm kidding, Livvie. I love my babies, and I wouldn't change a thing that brought you both to me. I'm just saying you two have plenty of time to figure everything out, and at least the sex can't lead to an accident that keeps you together, eh?"

The wink her mom threw Ruth's way was missed by Ruth, since her concerned face was staring at Olivia. Or, *an accident*, as her mother apparently liked to call her. Both sets of eyes were on Olivia, and she knew her reaction right now would pave the tone for the rest of this trip. She could react how she wanted to, meet fire with fire, and tell her mom that she hadn't exactly been enough to keep her dad with them anyway. But no, that wasn't her role in this game they played. Olivia defused, she diverted, she fixed.

"As enjoyable as talking with my mother about the benefits of my sex life has been, we've got things we need to get done before we hit the road again tomorrow. So do you want to talk now, or later?"

Olivia's anticipation at what her mom wanted to discuss had slowly ebbed. From the way the conversation had gone so far, Olivia suspected Grace had let something slip about her love life, and that's what had prompted this urgent trip.

Her mom looked crestfallen as she asked, "You're only staying one night? Can't you stay a little longer, especially if you have other things to do? I have the room all made up and I made stew for tonight, your favourite."

The familiar thread of guilt weaved its way around Olivia's stomach. She hated saying no to her mom, even if the logical part of her knew that the request was nothing more than another tool of manipulation. Olivia had already told her mom she'd only be staying one night. Making the trip at all left her worrying about leaving Grace alone with Henry, considering his worsening state. Whichever way Olivia turned, guilt followed.

Olivia opened her mouth to disappoint her mother, but Ruth beat her to it.

"I'm sorry, Ellen, that's my fault. I asked Ollie to accompany me while I visit my childhood home, not far from here. I didn't want to do it alone. And I need to get back tomorrow to finish up some work on my latest project."

Her mom pursed her lips, and Olivia waited for the curt

reply. Or worse, the questioning about Ruth's childhood, something Olivia suspected Ruth wasn't prepared to delve into. Her mom could be like a dog with a bone when her curiosity was piqued, other people's feelings be damned.

"That stew sounds great, though. What time is dinner? And do you have a favourite dessert? I'd love to pick something up while we're out to say thanks. I'm really grateful for the effort you've gone to."

Her mom's face melted into a smile and Olivia sighed in relief. Ruth's compliments held the right note of sincerity to avoid sounding contrived. They chatted about desserts for a moment on the way to the front door and Olivia squeezed Ruth's hand in gratitude. She had never made such an easy escape from her mom's, so whatever magic Ruth had, Olivia wanted to keep around.

CHAPTER TWELVE

Ruth's stomach flipped as they turned onto the road leading to her childhood home. She had no idea what to expect. The flashes of memories she occasionally got were fragmented and unclear. The houses were two-storey, semi-detached, not all that different to Ollie's childhood home. There were flares of personality here and there but none hugely indistinguishable from the next.

Ruth couldn't help comparing the difference between here and Wicker Hill, where no two homes were the same in the whole village. The residents were nothing if not individual, and their properties held clear stamps of personality before you set foot inside a door. Ollie pulled the car up in front of one of the houses and killed the engine. There was a glinting gold number plate beside the dark grey front door, and Ruth took a deep breath. They were here.

"Do you want to get out?" Ollie asked.

Ruth nodded but sat rooted to the spot as she took it in.

"Take your time, we have as long as you need." Ollie's voice was soft but came out loud in the quiet of the car and the otherwise empty street. There were no bikes strewn upon lawns, no neighbours chatting with cups of tea beside their doors, not even a dog barking somewhere in the distance. It was the middle of a school- and workday for most, but Ruth couldn't help drawing the parallels in her mind.

"I'm not sure what I expected. A sign maybe of what happened here, or some standout thing to show me that the loss was significant. It looks like all the other houses."

Ollie didn't reply and Ruth was grateful for that. She knew the facts. It had been twenty years since the fire, the house had obviously been rebuilt, and any signs of the devastation the fire had caused were gone. Superficially, at least. Ollie's hand gently covered Ruth's where it lay on her lap, and Ruth noticed her own hand was shaking. She shot a small smile at Ollie and took some more steadying breaths before nodding resolutely.

"I want to get out and look a little more. I came all this way. I feel like it's now or never. But I don't know what to do. Do I knock? What's the point? Surely whoever lives there now wouldn't have known my parents."

Ruth wasn't expecting Ollie to have answers, but it was good to speak her thoughts aloud rather than letting them rattle around in her head and build more uncertainty.

"Let's take it one step at a time. How about we just get out of the car first?"

Ruth found herself opening the door and moving at Ollie's suggestion, and she was grateful for the external prompting. She walked around and leaned against the car next to Ollie on the driver's side.

"I don't see a car in the drive. It doesn't look like anyone is home anyway. Maybe we should just go."

Ruth could hear the deflation in her own voice as she allowed her eyes to roam over the house, still hoping to spot something, anything, that would make this journey seem worthwhile.

"Look, someone's home next door."

Ruth turned her head toward where Ollie indicated and noticed the net curtain falling back into place.

"If anyone would've known your parents, it would be neighbours, right?"

Excitement was building in Ollie's voice as Ruth bit her lip anxiously. The thought of approaching a total stranger to ask about her deceased parents was terrifying. Her palms were already sweating, and her heart began to race. *What am I doing? Why am I here?* Ruth was overwhelmed with an urge to get away, far away. Anywhere but here.

Ruth dimly registered the door to the neighbour's house unlocking as she warred with an internal battle in her head while her feet stayed rooted to the spot. What caught her attention more was Ollie's movements. Ollie stood up from where they leaned against the car and moved toward the gated entrance to the house. Ruth followed Ollie with her eyes and saw a woman walking toward them. She looked friendly, if a little cautious, as she reached the gate. Ruth wondered what she must be thinking, seeing two women parked outside staring at her neighbour's house for what was more than enough time to make someone uncomfortable.

Ruth willed her feet to move, but her brain was too busy trying to keep her heart from losing control and reminding her lungs to breathe.

"Hi, sorry to bother you, we were going to knock but we weren't sure if anyone was home."

Ollie was speaking calmly and confidently. Her voice put the other woman at ease as she relaxed her stance and smiled at Ollie.

"No problem. I saw you out here and you looked a little lost, so I figured I'd see if you needed any help."

"Yeah, I'm Ollie and this is Ruth."

Ollie glanced back and Ruth willed herself to move

forward, act normal, don't scare this poor stranger. Ruth was grateful when Ollie picked up on some of the thoughts flitting through her head and walked closer. She reached out and gripped Ruth's hand to hold in hers. Ollie took a deep breath in and out as she looked into Ruth's eyes. Ruth mimicked the action and was immediately grateful for the influx of air she had been sorely needing. The rhythmic tapping of Ollie's fingers against hers registered and Ruth smiled. Ollie was using Ruth's own technique to calm, tapping her fingers in a pattern that grounded Ruth and brought her back quicker than even she would've thought possible.

"Thank you," Ruth whispered as she squeezed Ollie's hand.

Ruth looked past Ollie to the concerned woman's face. Ruth wanted to say something comforting to put the woman at ease, but she was still working on breathing right now. Luckily for her, Ollie turned and walked forward again, keeping Ruth's hand in hers as Ruth followed her lead.

"I'm sorry. We'd be grateful for your help. We were wondering if you perhaps knew the previous occupants of the house next door?"

Ollie nodded toward Ruth's childhood home, and the woman looked contemplative for a moment.

"Hmmm, not well, the last crowd kept to themselves quite a bit."

Ruth's heart sank as the woman spoke, ready to pack it all in and go back to her life. Ignorance was bliss and all, right?

"The Burke family, I think they were? They only lasted about a year, though, before it was sold again."

Ruth's head shot up again at that. *The Burke family, only a year.* She wasn't talking about Ruth's parents.

"No, sorry, I should've realized there might've been

several previous occupants. I'm talking about twenty years ago, there was a family that lived here. There was a fire and…"

Ollie trailed off as recognition flashed in the other woman's eyes and she looked sorrowful. She knew what happened. That much was clear. What else might she know? Her eyes flicked from Ollie to Ruth and her eyes widened a little. Ruth's breath hitched, and it seemed like an eternity of this stranger's eyes taking her in.

"Wait, Ruth? You said your name is Ruth?"

Ruth nodded slowly and the woman smiled while shaking her head slowly.

"Wow. You've grown so much. You're the image of your mother. I can't believe it's you. I've often wondered how you were doing."

The last sentence reverberated around Ruth's head as tears pricked at her eyes. The question she had asked herself so many times before now answered with three simple words. *I've often wondered.*

❖

Olivia's eyes bounced between Ruth and the stranger who was apparently not such a stranger to Ruth after all. This moment was monumental, and Olivia felt a little like just a spectator of this reunion. Ruth was clearly having trouble speaking, though, and the woman seemed to be waiting for a response or confirmation, so Olivia jumped in.

"Ruth came here hoping to find out some more about her parents. You knew them, then?"

The woman nodded and opened the gate to beckon them in.

"Come in, come in, I'll throw the kettle on, and we can

have a chat. It's been a while, but I haven't quite lost my memory yet, so I have plenty of stories to share."

Olivia kept hold of Ruth's hand, tapping the rhythm she hoped provided comfort as they were led inside the house. Olivia couldn't help thinking how it must be almost identical to the house Ruth spent her first years in, considering the whole estate looked like cookie cutter homes. Would it spark any memories for Ruth? Olivia hoped if it did, they were good. From her own scattered childhood memories, she knew that wasn't always a guarantee.

"I'm sorry, I haven't even introduced myself yet. I'm Nora. Take a seat there. Tea? Coffee?"

Olivia slid into a chair at the table Nora indicated and Ruth sat beside her. She glanced at Ruth briefly, then asked for tea for them both. Ruth looked like she needed a little longer to get her bearings, and Olivia was happy to be her voice as long as she needed.

"Thanks, Nora. I appreciate you giving us some of your time," Olivia said.

Nora set the cups down in front of them and sat across the table. Her eyes kept darting to Ruth with a soft, sad smile on her face all the while.

"Not at all, I love the company. My kids call when they can, but otherwise it's just me in this big house since my Dennis passed."

Nora looked up and Olivia followed her eyes to a family portrait on the wall. Nora stood, clearly happy, with Dennis by her side, and three kids of varying ages smiling brightly in front of them.

"I'm sorry for your loss. You have a beautiful family."

Nora nodded, pride evident in her smile and her words.

"That I do, I've been blessed many times over."

"You remember me?" Ruth's voice was hoarse, like speaking her first words after a deep sleep. Olivia was grateful to hear the sweet sound.

"Of course I do, little Roo."

The nickname made Ruth smile. It sparked something in Olivia's brain that she couldn't quite place. It sounded familiar, but why? Roo, like in Winnie-the-Pooh maybe? The comparisons were funny now, considering Ruth's comment about the Hundred Acre Wood from the other day. It must've been where Piglet got her name, too. Conflicting emotions crossed Ruth's face as she relaxed more into the seat.

"I wasn't really sure what I'd find when I got here. I just wanted to know more. About who I was before the fire, about my parents. Anything, really."

Nora nodded in understanding and reached a hand across to grip Ruth's. Ruth tensed for a moment at the gesture. It was a barely perceptible movement, one that Olivia wasn't sure even she would've recognized not all that long ago. Sometimes it felt like she had known Ruth forever, and other times little things reminded her that they'd barely begun this. Whatever this was. *Relationship? Adventure? Hiatus from reality?*

Not that last one, because there were too many daily reminders lately that slapped reality in her face. Truth was, despite the chaotic side quest her life had taken, Olivia had never before felt so grounded in reality as she was with Ruth.

"Let me grab them quickly, I won't be long."

Nora hopped up and headed for the stairs as Olivia tuned back into the conversation. Olivia had been lost in her own thoughts while they spoke, but Ruth had a soft smile on her face as Olivia took her in. Ruth answered Olivia's unspoken question about what Nora was going to grab.

"I can't believe she still has photos. My parents were so

young in their wedding photo that I have, I've never even seen what they looked like at my age."

The mixture of excitement and sadness in Ruth's tone pulled at Olivia's heart, and she couldn't stop herself from reaching out to place a soft kiss against Ruth's lips. Olivia pulled back as Nora walked back into the room and gave them a sweet smile.

"Young love. It's one of life's greatest gifts, so make sure you two cherish it."

Olivia's cheeks heated a little as she grinned sheepishly. Nora set down an old album in front of them. It looked like one of a set similar to albums her grandmother used to have.

Nora flipped the pages until she landed on one and pointed to a picture on a page of six. "That was my Deirdre's third birthday. You two would've been around the same age."

Olivia watched Ruth looking at the photo. A soft, silent tear trailed down Ruth's face as Olivia looked at the picture for herself. The old image was of a tall man, around the same age as Olivia was now, if she had to guess. He had his arm around a woman, and Olivia did a double take because Nora had been right, it was like looking at Ruth. The woman had Ruth's same sparkling blue eyes. She looked similar in height to Ruth and her smile was a mirror image of the one that made Olivia's heart flip daily. In the photo, that smile was duplicated by a little girl in a pink dress who sat comfortably on the woman's hip. *Ruth.*

Ruth traced a finger over the plastic sleeve that housed the precious photo. Nora reached over and slipped the photo out of its pocket and handed it to Ruth, who held it with a feather light touch. The tears fell more freely now as Ruth took in every inch of the image while Olivia watched her.

"What were their names?" Olivia asked in a quiet voice. It occurred to her she didn't know, and that seemed like a big thing not to know about the woman she loved. *Hold up. Did I really just think that?* Olivia glanced at Ruth, suddenly worried that she had somehow said it out loud. It was far too soon to be thinking that, never mind speaking it.

"Kate and Cormac." Ruth spoke the words tentatively, as if they hadn't passed her lips in a long time. "That dress is hideous."

Ruth laughed as she pointed to the younger version of herself. Olivia chuckled and nodded in agreement. It was a terrible dress.

"My kids say the same when they look at the outfits I had them in. It was all the style back then. I'm sure Deirdre had that exact dress as well. We used to match you two sometimes. Your mom said it reminded her of when she was young and how much she hated being matched with her sister. Greta loved it, of course. She idolized Kate when they were little."

Nora's smile fell at that, and she shook her head sadly. Olivia wondered if the conversation was bringing back up Nora's own grief. She must've been pretty close to Kate if they matched their kids' outfits and were next door neighbours.

"You know my aunt?" Ruth asked.

"I did. We lived next door to each other all our young lives. My parents passed this house to me, and your grandparents did the same for Kate. I was older than Kate when we were kids, so of course I was too cool for her." Nora laughed lightly. "But we grew closer when we both settled down here again."

Ruth hung on every word Nora spoke, and Olivia's heart ached for her. She could tell how badly Ruth needed to hear about her parents, about her life before Wicker Hill.

"Greta doesn't talk about them much. My parents. I don't really know anyone else who knew them, so this means a lot," Ruth said.

"It must be hard for her. I was never happy about what

happened there. It was hard for your mom, too. Kate wouldn't talk about it much, but I always hoped they'd reconcile someday. I'm sure neither of them imagined they'd run out of time so soon," Nora said.

Ruth frowned and Olivia suddenly wanted to stop the conversation before it went any further. It was important for Ruth to understand more about her parents and the life she had come from, but Olivia hoped it wouldn't somehow cost her the one she had now. It was clear there was a reason Ruth didn't remember Greta before her parents died, and Olivia wasn't sure a stranger was the person who should be telling her.

"What part weren't you happy about?" Ruth asked tentatively.

"Well, it's just you know, when Greta was caught kissing that girl, it wasn't a surprise her parents weren't happy about it. Not that it's any excuse, but it was more of a shock back then than it is now. But kicking her out like they did was too far, I always said."

Olivia's stomach dropped, and by the look on Ruth's face, hers did the same.

"I don't know all the ins and outs—your mom never spoke about it. But I will never understand that poor girl losing her family just for loving someone. I hope she's doing okay now. I always had time for her."

For all her family's faults, one thing Olivia never had to experience was the fear of losing them for being a lesbian. She was grateful to never have had that worry while discovering who she was. She couldn't imagine the pain that came from choosing between your parents or yourself.

"Excuse me, please." Ruth's voice was shaky as she got up from the table and walked toward the front door. Olivia stood to follow, and Nora looked at her apologetically.

"I'm sorry. I said too much," Nora said.

Olivia wanted to get to Ruth and make sure she was okay. But they also came into Nora's life out of nowhere and brought up a grief she had likely made peace with already. Nora might be the closest thing Ruth had to a link to her parents, and Olivia wanted to make sure that link was still available when she needed it again.

"No, it's not you. Ruth has struggled not knowing much, and I think it's all a little overwhelming. But you've given her a gift today, so thank you. Do you mind if I maybe get your number, in case she feels like chatting some more? Only if that's okay with you."

Nora grabbed an envelope and pen from a drawer and wrote a landline and mobile number on it. So, other people did still have landlines then. As Olivia waited, keeping one eye on the door, Nora pulled a few photos from other pages and placed them inside the envelope.

"You tell Roo to call me anytime."

Olivia smiled and took the envelope, thanking Nora again before she walked toward the door. She took a quick look at the top photo of the pile. A little girl stood in front of a fresh cream birthday cake with *Happy 6th Birthday Ruth* in chocolate icing on top. The image made her pause. The itching in her head of a memory trying to form resurfaced. Suddenly, it hit Olivia, and she was transported back to all those years ago in the hospital.

The girl who didn't speak yet had managed to make Olivia feel more understood than anyone in her short life up until that point. The girl who was there one day and gone the next, leaving nothing but a drawing to remind Olivia. A drawing that still sat in a box in the room of the house they were about to return to, with two scrawled words across the bottom of the page.

Livy and Roo.

CHAPTER THIRTEEN

Ruth sat in the car and focused on breathing in and out as the world swam around her. Her tear-filled eyes made everything look hazy, and the ringing in her ears almost drowned out the thumping of her heart.

You're safe. Keep breathing. This will pass. It always does. You're safe.

Ruth spoke the words to herself like a mantra, as reminders of the things her body needed to believe to calm her nervous system. Her thumb touched each finger over and over as the ringing in her ears ebbed to a bearable volume and each breath came a little easier than the last.

See, you're almost there. Breathe in, breathe out, that's your only job right now.

Funny how the voice in her head was still that of her therapist, whom she definitely needed to make another appointment with. Therapy gave her tools and tips and words to use, but it didn't magically make the anxiety disappear, which was a fact that Ruth resented in moments like these. Even the medication she took had its limitations. While she would be forever grateful to have those supports in place, they didn't stop the panic attacks completely. They did, however, give her a better chance at being able to recognize the symptoms early and deal with them.

The driver's side door opened, and Ollie slid in beside her.

"Are you okay? I'm sorry I took so long," Ollie said.

Had she? Ruth wasn't sure how much time had passed since she had gotten to the car. Her plan had been to get some air and return. But when she walked outside and her thoughts spiralled with the words Nora had spoken, air wasn't coming quite as easily as she'd hoped. Thankfully, they had left the car door unlocked and Ruth retreated to the relative safety of the enclosed space to ride it out.

"Ruth?"

Ollie's concerned voice penetrated her racing thoughts, and Ruth was distantly aware of the feeling of Ollie's fingers tapping gently against her hand. Ruth focused on the pattern and relaxed into Ollie's touch, still unable to offer words to ease Ollie's concerns.

Ollie broke the momentary silence with an off-key rendition of the first line of "I Will Survive," and Ruth's head shot up in surprise. It was so random that Ruth stared in shock for a moment while Ollie continued both the singing and the tapping on her hand. As Ollie got to the part where the beat kicked in and started drumming with her other hand against the dashboard Ruth broke into fits of laughter. That didn't deter Ollie, who continued the song like it was her final audition on one of those reality TV shows, as tears streamed down Ruth's face.

What a sight they must've been for anyone passing. Two women sitting in the car on a suburban estate, one crying from a combination of post anxiety attack exhaustion and laughter and the other doing an absurd performance that now included foot tapping and facial expressions. As Ollie finished the final notes, Ruth leaned over to kiss her softly.

"Thank you."

The two words felt too insignificant, too small, to convey

the depth of Ruth's gratitude. Not only for serenading her and returning her heart to its normal beat, but for being there through all of it today. Ruth had so much to process, and she knew it would take time to sift through it all and figure out what it meant. But right now, she wanted to focus on everything this beautiful woman had brought to her life.

Ruth took out her phone and turned it to selfie mode. She held it out and smiled at Ollie as she pressed the screen to take the photo. Ollie leaned in to press another kiss against her lips, and Ruth kept clicking. Ollie's influence on her life might not be visible in the images, but her heart was full, and she wanted to capture every moment, tear-stained cheeks and all.

❖

Dinner with Ollie's mom had been mostly, thankfully, uneventful. The stew was amazing, and Ollie and her mom played nicer than they had at lunch. There was so much beneath the surface there that Ruth wanted to unpack, but she was too exhausted to start doing that now. The only semi-argument that had broken out was when Ollie informed Ellen, and Ruth for that matter, that she had booked a hotel room for the night. Ellen had clearly been offended at the idea that they wouldn't be staying with her as she had planned. There were several back-and-forths between the pair while Ruth watched on, and eventually Ollie promised to drop by for lunch before heading back to Wicker Hill the next day.

"We could've stayed at your mom's place," Ruth said as they made the short distance to a four-star chain hotel.

"We could have. But it's been a long day, and we both need to recharge. The thought of doing that in a hotel alone with you was too appealing to pass up," Ollie replied.

Ruth wasn't going to complain, because the idea of being

alone in a hotel room with Ollie wasn't something to complain about. When Ollie opened the door to the room, Ruth's stomach flipped at the sight of the king-sized bed. Images flashed through her mind of all the things she wanted to do with Ollie on that bed at the same time as a loud yawn made its way out of her mouth.

"You're exhausted, darling." Ollie spoke the words gently, like you do when dealing with an overtired toddler who missed their nap. Ruth found herself reacting like one, too, frowning at the words and resistant to the idea of sleep robbing all the time for fun.

"It's barely eight. There's plenty of time left in the evening."

Ruth's body protested her words as the full force of the day hit her at once. She sat on the edge of the bed and willed herself not to cry again. She was in a beautiful hotel room with her beautiful girlfriend for the first time, and the last thing she wanted to do was waste the night on more tears.

The bed sank beside her as Ollie sat down. She cupped Ruth's face with a soft hand and guided Ruth's eyes up to meet hers.

"How about a bath?" Ollie asked.

Ruth smiled and nodded, hoping her eyes didn't give away exactly how tired she was. She didn't want Ollie treating her with kid gloves, but she wasn't sure exactly how much she had to give right now.

"You turn on the TV and see if there's anything good for us to watch after, and I'll get the bath ready, okay?"

Ruth nodded again. Talking sometimes took too much precious energy, and she was grateful that Ollie accepted that. Not only accepted, but understood, too. It had Ruth's throat filling with words she wasn't yet ready to say. She swallowed them down and moved to grab the remote control as Ollie made her way to the bathroom. Ruth flicked through the channels and landed on one that would be playing *Coyote Ugly* in about an hour. Nothing was going to beat that.

Ollie called for her as Ruth heard the taps shut off. The overhead light was off and there was a soft glow from the mirror light along with a lamp Ollie must've pulled in from the desk. The bath was full to the brim with bubbles, and Ruth smiled at the sight. Ollie stepped toward her and gripped the end of Ruth's T-shirt, tugging it up as Ruth lifted her arms. Slowly and carefully, Ollie helped strip Ruth of every inch of her clothing until Ruth stood naked in front of a far too clothed Ollie.

"Your turn," Ruth said softly.

Ollie shook her head slowly and Ruth's smile dropped.

"I wanted to run it for you, so you can unwind before sleep. I can see how tired you are, darling. Let me take care of you tonight," Ollie said.

Ruth leaned up and placed a soft kiss on Ollie's lips. Ollie's breath hitched as Ruth's breasts grazed against her thin shirt.

"You can take care of me. In there. If I'm that tired, it would be irresponsible to leave me unattended in water, don't you think?"

Ruth bit her lip and shrugged as Ollie closed her eyes with a sigh. Ruth hoped Ollie was losing whatever resolve she thought she had. Ollie's clothes were off in record time, and Ruth drank in every inch of her body as an ache began between her legs. Ollie slid into the hot water and held a hand out for Ruth to do the same. Ruth settled between Ollie's legs and pressed her back to Ollie's bare breasts as gentle arms wrapped around her from behind.

"This is much better than being alone," Ruth murmured as Ollie's hands stroked her skin softly beneath the bubbles.

"I was trying to be chivalrous and make sure you knew I was okay with whatever you needed tonight. I don't want any pressure between us. Being with you is enough, sex doesn't need to be on the cards."

Ruth placed a hand over Ollie's and led Ollie's hand down farther to her pulsing core. She leaned her head back against Ollie's neck and whispered soft words in her ear as Ollie's heart thumped against her back.

"But what if I want it to be?"

❖

Olivia groaned and kissed the nape of Ruth's neck as she worked her fingers between Ruth's folds, massaging gently. Ruth whimpered quietly as Olivia kissed her way up to Ruth's ear. Olivia pressed her fingers lower until she reached Ruth's entrance. She hesitated briefly before whispering softly in Ruth's ear, "Are you sure?"

Ruth pressed her hand above Olivia's again and guided Olivia's fingers inside her in answer. The action sent a lightning bolt of lust to Olivia's clit. She pressed two fingers deeper into Ruth, and the action moved Ruth's ass back more against Olivia's already aching centre. Olivia moved her other hand up in search of Ruth's breast as her lips made their way to the other side of Ruth's neck.

Olivia teased Ruth's nipple between her thumb and forefinger and picked up the pace of her hand, massaging Ruth's clit with her palm on every thrust. Ruth's quiet whimpers quickly turned to moans as she reached a hand back to grip the back of Olivia's head.

"Please, fuck…"

The words were more forceful than pleading, and Olivia

curled her fingers in response to apply more pressure where Ruth needed it. She massaged the hardened nipple between her fingers and grazed her teeth lightly along the sensitive nape of Ruth's neck. Ruth's legs clenched and her head fell back as she gasped and shook. Olivia held her tightly until her body relaxed back and Ruth tilted her head to kiss Olivia's lips.

Olivia stroked Ruth's hair gently as they stared at each other in silence. Despite the throbbing between her legs, nothing in the world was more important than taking in the universe in Ruth's eyes at that moment. Olivia smiled as Ruth's eyelids drooped and then flew back open as she tried to fight the tiredness pulling her under.

"Let's go to bed, darling," Olivia said gently with her arms still wrapped tightly around Ruth. Ruth nodded but made no effort to move apart from resting her head against Olivia's chest.

"You're going to fall asleep on me, and although I have no complaints about that, the location isn't ideal."

Ruth gave a small smile and pressed a soft kiss against Olivia's chest right above her heart, which began beating more rapidly with Ruth's lips against her skin. There were so many places Olivia wanted those lips to explore, but right now her priority was Ruth getting the rest she clearly needed.

"More of that after you've rested. In bed," Olivia added, in case Ruth decided to get comfortable against her chest again. Olivia wasn't sure how much more she could take before her body screamed for relief.

"Hmph. Fine," Ruth grumbled. She moved enough to let Olivia slip out of the now cooling water. Olivia grabbed the two towels that she had set aside earlier and wrapped one around herself before she reached to help for Ruth. Ruth stepped out of the tub on shaky legs, and Olivia had to bite back a groan that almost got loose at the sight of Ruth's curves. Partly to give her wandering eyes a break, Olivia wrapped the remaining towel around Ruth and smiled at the yawn that escaped her.

"It's been a long day," Olivia said.

"Mm-hmm. Anxiety attacks can leave me drained. It's like the energy it takes to get through them zaps everything from me sometimes. But I don't want to waste the time we have here sleeping. Maybe if I rest a little—"

Olivia placed a finger over Ruth's lips to quieten her whispered words. She cupped Ruth's face gently and stroked Ruth's cheek with her thumb.

"Being here with you isn't a waste of time. I'm not going to tell you not to worry, because I know that's not helpful. But look in my eyes and trust me when I say that even if all we do is lie in that super-comfy looking bed and sleep together, I would never call that a waste."

Ruth looked into Olivia's eyes for a moment before she leaned up to kiss her again.

"How did I find you, Ollie? It's all too perfect. You need to add this to the list of fairy-tale moments."

You found me twenty years ago when you had lost everything else.

Olivia spoke the words in her head because she was sure that now was not the time to spring more information on Ruth. Olivia was still processing it herself, and although it made this adventure of theirs all the more fairy-tale-like, she didn't want to overload Ruth with more things about her past that Ruth didn't recall.

"If this is all it takes, that list is going to fill up very quickly," Olivia replied as they both got dry and headed out to the waiting bed.

"Promises, promises," Ruth murmured.

Olivia glanced toward their bags where her pyjamas sat, wondering if she should grab them. Ruth pulled back the covers of the bed and slid beneath them naked as if answering Olivia's unspoken question. Olivia joined her and shivered at the feel of the cool duvet against her bare skin. Ruth reached a hand across to rub Olivia's arm, which heated far more places on Olivia's body than where Ruth's palm connected.

"Is *Coyote Ugly* on yet?" Ruth said as she moved closer. Olivia smiled at the sleepy voice and moved an arm out for Ruth to slide beneath. She glanced toward the soft glow of the television where the main character was entering the meet-cute stage of her journey.

"Yep. No dancing yet, so you haven't missed too much."

When she was met with no response, Olivia glanced down at a sleeping Ruth curled against her side. She ran her fingers up and down Ruth's back and placed a gentle kiss on the top of her head. Ruth hummed softly and wrapped an arm around Olivia's waist to cuddle even closer. Olivia turned back to watch the scenes unfold on screen, but her brain wasn't cooperating with the distraction technique.

Every part of her body was hyperaware of Ruth's body pressed against hers. But that wasn't what was keeping her from focusing on the movie. It was the slow, steady beating of her own heart that had Olivia's mind working overtime. This woman curled beneath her arm had ripped open a part of Olivia she had sworn was sealed tightly away. Olivia had seen what relationships, what love, could do.

Her parents had almost destroyed each other, and Olivia had got caught in the crossfire. Then, after she had found her feet away from her childhood home, her last relationship had taken every bit of stability she had built for herself. Now, here Olivia was, falling head over heels in love so quickly, in a way she was sure she had never experienced before. Olivia could already tell the difference in the depth of her feelings for Ruth. *Who am I kidding?* There was nowhere left to fall. Olivia was well and truly already there.

CHAPTER FOURTEEN

The thigh pressed firmly between Ruth's legs when she woke explained the vivid dreams she was having. Dreams featuring Olivia, who lay naked beside her. Ruth was sure as she looked at Ollie's sleeping face that no dream in the world could compare to waking up like this every day.

Ruth was more than aware that she had fallen asleep last night before she repaid Ollie for taking care of her in more ways than one. Although she was comfortable Ollie wasn't keeping tabs, there was nothing Ruth wanted more in that moment than to repay her. She ran a finger slowly down Ollie's cheek and watched her eyelids flutter open to reveal beautiful green eyes.

"I'm sorry for waking you. Well, I'm not, because we haven't yet had the discussion on whether you consent to me touching you in your sleep. So, I needed you awake to do what I really, really want to do."

Ollie's mouth fell open, and a soft groan escaped her lips as Ruth smiled. She enjoyed taking Ollie by surprise, or taking her, full stop. Ruth stroked Ollie's cheek again slowly, deliberately, loving the way it made Ollie's gaze soften in response.

"So, are you awake enough to give me your blessing?"

Ruth was teasing now, since the blatant lust was obvious on Ollie's face.

"Let's state right now that unless I say otherwise in advance, if we're naked in bed together, then you have my full permission to touch me any damn way you please."

Ollie pressed her knee more firmly between Ruth's legs as she spoke the words in a near growl.

"Definitely noted," Ruth replied as she pushed Ollie onto her back and straddled her hips.

"Fuck, you look hot," Ollie said as she caressed Ruth's bare breasts. Ruth gripped her wrist and placed it above Ollie's head. Surprise flashed through Ollie's eyes, and she grinned as Ruth placed her hand over Ollie's other wrist. She held both to the bed while she leaned down and brushed a kiss across Ollie's lips.

"You took very, very good care of me last night. It's my turn to take care of you, okay?"

Ollie audibly gulped and nodded as Ruth kissed her way down Ollie's chest. She placed soft, open mouthed kisses in circles around Ollie's nipple before pulling it between her lips and sucking gently. Ollie gasped and arched against her mouth as Ruth moved to the other side, paying the same careful attention to Ollie's other nipple.

"You feel so damn good." Ollie's voice was hoarse as she reached a hand up to the back of Ruth's head. Ruth stopped what she was doing and pulled back, placing Ollie's hand beside her head on the bed once more. She shook her head in mock disapproval.

"Your hands stay there. Just relax and enjoy."

Ollie's frown melted into a moan as Ruth batted her eyelashes and applied pressure to her nipple with her fingers as she spoke again. "Please?"

"Yes. Shit, yes." Ollie nodded to emphasize her point, and Ruth got back to her slow exploration of Ollie's body. After making her way down past Ollie's hips and settling between her thighs, Ruth's effect on Ollie was evident. Ruth flicked her tongue out to taste the glistening wetness that waited for her. Ollie's moans grew louder as she gripped the sheets in desperation.

"Please, darling, I need you," Ollie panted out.

Ruth parted Ollie's lips and ran her tongue around the sweet, sensitive flesh. She kissed and licked everywhere except the one place Ollie needed her most. Ruth raised her eyes to look up at Ollie, whose face was an exquisite mixture of pleasure and frustration. She kept her eyes trained on Ollie's face as she wrapped her lips around Ollie's aching clit and sucked.

"Fuck, yes, there." Ollie's voice was huskier than usual, and Ruth felt the words across every inch of her own skin. She applied more pressure with her tongue and gripped Ollie's thighs to hold her in place. Having taken her time getting there, Ruth was in no hurry to leave. She alternated her movements and pulled back on the pressure when she sensed Ollie getting near the brink. Finally, unable to hold back any longer, Ruth kept a steady rhythm with her tongue until Ollie's legs shot out straight and she let out a guttural cry.

Ollie's body went limp beneath Ruth's, and Ruth placed soft kisses on Ollie's inner thigh.

"Do I get to touch you now, darling?" Ollie murmured.

Ruth's body screamed *Yes please* as she warred between her desire to stay between Ollie's legs and her desire to find the release she desperately craved. Then again, why was she choosing at all?

"I'm not done with you yet, but"—Ruth paused as she

straddled Ollie's hips again and faced the opposite direction this time, before looking over her shoulder to continue—"I think we can both get what we want, don't you?"

Ollie stared back with a salacious smile and nodded. She reached forward to grip Ruth's hips and guided her back until her hot breath was between Ruth's legs. Ruth was already so turned on from watching Ollie writhe beneath her that she was worried it would be over before it even began. She focused her attention back between Ollie's legs and ran a finger up and down the still sensitive flesh as Ollie twitched beneath her.

"You're already soaked. It's hot as fuck," Ollie said as she ran a finger over Ruth in the same way.

"Your body does that to me, especially when it's beneath my lips." Ruth gasped as the last word left her mouth. Ollie explored every available inch of Ruth with her tongue, as she gripped Ruth's thighs with her arms. Ruth got lost in the flooding of sensations coursing through her body as she pressed back to get more. She soon realized Ollie was repaying her for the extended teasing as Ollie's tongue moved every time Ruth got too close.

"Ollie, please, more." Ruth panted as the vibrations of Ollie's satisfied murmur rippled through her body.

"Who needs patience now, hmm?" Ollie spoke in between teasing kisses and Ruth bit back a retort. She smiled to herself as she refocused on her initial goal. The best way to get her own release was to make damn sure Ollie couldn't hold back. Ruth teased Ollie's opening gently and leaned in to place a soft kiss against Ollie's swollen clit.

"I can be patient. I'll find a way to keep myself occupied," Ruth said before she wrapped her lips around the sensitive clit and sucked. She pushed two fingers inside Ollie and felt more than heard Ollie's responding groan. Ollie gripped her ass and pushed her tongue inside Ruth, moving it in tandem with Ruth's finger strokes. Ollie reached a finger up to apply a steady pressure to Ruth's clit as she kept pace with her tongue, and Ruth saw stars.

Ruth's own body was so close to the edge as she kept up the movement of her fingers and tongue. Right as Ollie clenched around her fingers and her legs began to shake, Ruth erupted in waves of her own pleasure rippling through her body. As the last of the waves ebbed, Ruth turned to bring her face up to Ollie's and kissed her gently. Ollie wrapped still shaking arms around Ruth and ran her fingers over Ruth's spine in a soothing motion.

Ruth pulled the blanket back over them and laid her head against Ollie's chest. The steady pounding of Ollie's heart combined with the trailing of Ollie's fingers created a comforting cocoon that Ruth never wanted to leave.

"Can we stay like this forever?" Ruth whispered softly, only partly joking. The silence stretched between them for a few moments and Ruth wondered if Ollie had fallen asleep already. Her eyes were closed, and she could feel her own satiated tiredness pulling her under when the soft reply came.

"Promises, promises," Ollie whispered.

❖

"So, what did your mom need to actually talk to you about?"

They were in the car on the way back to Wicker Hill after a surprisingly pleasant lunch at her mom's house. Olivia loved her mom, truly, but it was rare she went a whole meal without the familiar frustration or guilt rising from one sly remark or another.

"She said she was worried about me, and that Grace told her I wasn't acting like myself. As if I could be expected to, given the circumstances. I'd bet my life on the fact that Grace only said anything after much prompting, and my mom grabbed that as an excuse to demand to see me."

Silence stretched between them for a moment before Ruth spoke again.

"It must be hard for her, seeing you both up there with Mr B. after everything that happened. From the bits and pieces you've told me, it's not a surprise she'd be worried about you."

Something twisted in Olivia's gut, and she swallowed back her immediate dismissive retort. She could understand how it looked to Ruth, but from years of dealing with her mother's emotional manipulation, it wasn't that black and white.

"My mom always has a reason to urgently need me, and I'm expected to drop everything and go to her the minute that happens."

"Do you think she's lonely, maybe?" Ruth asked.

The question was innocent and didn't call for the anger that began bubbling in Olivia's stomach. The feeling had nothing to do with Ruth, and everything to do with years of guilt and pressure and similar remarks from less well-meaning people. *She's lonely, she misses you, she's your mother. He's trying, he misses you, he's your father.* There was always a reason why her parent's burdens should be hers to bear, regardless of the burdens they'd already passed along to her.

"My dad is dying and I'm already dealing with that. She's the parent, she should be supporting me, not expecting more from me right now." Olivia's words came out harsher than she intended, and she sighed in annoyance at herself. "Sorry, I'm a little wound up."

"That's the first time I've heard you call him that," Ruth said.

"What?" Olivia asked, even though she already knew the answer. The words had fallen out of her mouth before she could purposefully correct herself. Another brick in her wall crumbling down.

"Your dad," Ruth clarified.

"Yes, well, I worked hard on not thinking of him as such. Which was a lot easier when he wasn't around."

Olivia hated the bitterness in her voice. She hated the tears that prickled at the corners of her eyes. She hated that she didn't hate Henry quite as much as she used to. Seeing the frail, tired man whose body was punishing him far more than Olivia ever could left her with a sadness she couldn't quite resolve. And the time for resolutions was quickly slipping away.

"Do you think he's changed? Does that make a difference for you? Obviously, I only know him as who he was since coming to Wicker Hill. I can't really picture anything else."

Lucky you. Olivia spoke the words in her head but took time to consider what she wanted to say.

"He's changed. I don't really believe that his life now is all an act. He has been a great father to Grace. And he tried with me, but too little, too late. I was too old to forget the way Grace could."

Olivia blinked back tears as she opened wounds that had been slowly unravelling since she landed in Wicker Hill.

"Grace was very sick as a kid. My mom spent most of her time at appointments with doctors and hospitals. Instead of being there to support us all, Henry was out getting drunk and sleeping around and spending all the money we needed to survive."

The sleeping around part was seared into her brain from one of the many screaming matches she had witnessed between her parents while sitting on the stairs of their home.

"One time he didn't show up to collect me from school. My mom was in the hospital with Grace. One of the other parents dropped me home and I walked into the house to see him passed out on the couch with a bottle smashed on the floor. It must've fallen from his hands. I couldn't wake him no matter how much I tried, and I thought he was dead. He was just lying there, and he wouldn't move."

Ruth squeezed Olivia's hand as she took a breath before speaking again.

"I rang my mom, and I was crying and saying he was dead, and she sent an ambulance. I remember seeing blood on my hands and trying to find where he was bleeding. But it wasn't him, it was me. I cut myself on the glass trying to wake him and I barely even noticed. The ambulance came and they brought him to the hospital, and he was fine. Physically, anyway. But he never came home again after that. I went to the hospital every day after school instead and helped my mom with Grace, and we got by. We got by without him, better than we ever did with."

That last part was only partially true, but it was as much as Olivia could give right then. The real truth that she kept shoved deep down inside was from before Henry stopped being her dad. The times she remembered him singing to her, reading to her, telling her stories, and bringing her on adventures. Those were the real memories that needed to stay hidden. Those truths were much more painful to recall than the bad times. They were the ones that left Olivia with an aching desire for something she couldn't ever have again. Anger was far easier to deal with.

"I'm really sorry, Ollie. That must have been terrifying. I can imagine that must come up for you a lot now, considering—"

"Considering there's a very real possibility I will walk in, and he will be dead someday soon?"

"Yeah, that. Have you had a chance to talk to him about

anything? Getting some of it out might help, while you have time," Ruth said.

"And say what? Sorry you're dying but here are all the ways you fucked me up that maybe you don't even remember because you were blacked out for half of them? Sorry that when you did get your shit together, I was too angry and missed out on any possible chance of having a father, while I resented my little sister for getting the best parts of you? Sorry I wasn't good enough for you to want to get better for in the first place?"

Hot, angry tears trailed their way down Olivia's face as she swiped at them furiously. She was surprised to find that they were already nearing Ruth's cottage. She pulled the car in but left the engine running as Ruth turned toward her.

"If that's what you need to say, then say it. Say all of that, or some of it, or write it down so you can get your thoughts out in the way you need, and then read the parts you want to him. I know he'd rather hear that than nothing from you."

He'd rather. There it was again. *Olivia better hurry up and fix things so he can get what he needs before he dies.*

"Why am I always the one that has to fix things? Address my shit so I can be a better person for all these people who never did that for me."

"That's not what I'm saying. But…he did do that, though, right? I completely understand why you couldn't see that then because it all seemed too late. But can you see it now, that he did try to be a better person? Maybe he deserves—"

"What about what I fucking deserved?"

The words exploded from Olivia's mouth before she could claw them back, and the look on Ruth's face gutted her. Not fear, not even anger, but pity. Ruth was pitying her. Olivia couldn't exactly blame her. She was the one crying in her car about a father who hadn't done a thing wrong to her in almost two decades. Who Ruth only knew as the friendly neighbourhood postman. But the pity was like fuel to her flaming anger that disguised so much shame beneath.

"You deserved better. But maybe right now you deserve a chance to find some closure. I don't want you regretting anything. After everything I've heard this weekend, I would give anything to be able to talk to my parents and find out some truths, but I can't. I don't have that choice. Right now, you still do."

"That's not fair. Your parents didn't abandon you. They died. And telling me to appreciate the chance I have because you don't is bullshit. I get that *Mr B.* is practically royalty in this fucking village, but the man you know isn't my father. And the faster I can get away from this damn place and the people who judge me for the choices I was forced to make because of *him*, the better."

Ruth looked like she had been slapped and nodded solemnly in reply. She got out of the car to grab her bag and paused for a moment, but Olivia was too angry to speak. She wasn't angry at Ruth, not even at Henry. It was an untamed anger with no direction that she was terrified would destroy anything in its path if she opened her mouth again. Olivia stayed silent and watched Ruth walk away from her until the door closed and she was alone with her memories.

Chapter Fifteen

I t went from a fairy tale to a disaster so quickly I barely know how we got there, Soph."

Ruth sat on Sophie's couch in her cosiest pyjamas with a tub of mint chocolate chip ice cream in hand. After she'd walked into the empty cottage earlier and sighed in relief at the fact that Greta wasn't home, Ruth realized she wasn't in any state to face Greta with the new information she had right now. She had grabbed her already packed bag, with her unworn pyjamas, and showed up at Sophie's to stay for the night.

"It sounds like the visit with her mom brought a lot of stuff up for Ollie, and you got the brunt of that. Which sucks, and you don't deserve to be the target for anyone's unhealed shit. But, although you're always my priority here, I can't imagine the stress she's under right now. It wasn't about you, my love."

Ruth knew that already, but it didn't help shake the sadness from what Ollie had said.

"I know it's not about me, I do. But she basically said she can't wait to get away from this place and everyone in it. That includes me."

"Knowing it's not about you means you need to really believe it, Ruthie. She said something in anger because this place makes her face things she doesn't want to have to face. That doesn't mean she doesn't want to be with you. We're not going to catastrophize and turn this into a big miscommunication blowup, understand? That trope has no place in your fairy tale. We're all about open communication here, my love."

"Tell that to my aunt," Ruth grumbled.

She had given Sophie the play-by-play of the whole weekend, including the new information about Greta, her mom, and her grandparents in one rambling sweep. That had led to ice cream, pyjamas, and a talk-it-out fest, as so declared by Sophie.

"You mean your aunt who was ostracized from her family for kissing a girl, at what must have already been a super confusing time for her, then had to fend for herself from the ripe old age of sixteen. All of that was before she became guardian to a traumatized, anxiety ridden, orphaned six-year-old and had to try to make it up as she went along without knowing what she should or shouldn't say? If anyone gets forgiven for lack of open communication, it's her."

Ruth sighed while marvelling at Sophie's unique ability to put things in perspective without making Ruth feel judged.

"Once again, Greta can do no wrong in your eyes."

Sophie shrugged, not even pretending to refute the statement.

"I had this image in my head of my parents, and now I can't help thinking that maybe they wouldn't be proud of who I am. Maybe they would've turned their backs on me like my grandparents did to Greta. And I can't actually ask them. I have no way of knowing that at all, so I'm left with only these maybes. I don't want that for Ollie, too, you know? I don't want her to be left with maybes about her dad when he dies, instead of doing something about it while she has this chance."

Sophie shook her head and pointed her spoon at Ruth to

emphasize her disapproval while she finished the ice cream in her mouth.

"You're comparing incomparable things and you're twisting up your own shit with Ollie's. Her dad is going to die soon, that's a fact. Maybe she'll find ways to make peace with their past before that happens. Maybe she won't, and she'll need to find ways to do it afterward. Either way, she needs support, however *she* decides to deal with it. To be able to provide that, you need to keep it separate from your own baggage."

Ruth huffed and furrowed her brow. "When exactly did you get so wise? It's annoying."

"Years of therapy, my love. Turns out deep diving into understanding yourself gives you more skills to understand other people, too. Who knew?"

"Well, can we stop with the logical therapy and watch crappy movies with people who make bad decisions and still wind up happy until I fall asleep instead? Or is that beneath you now that you're all enlightened and stuff?"

Sophie grabbed the remote and tossed it to Ruth as she hopped up from the couch.

"Therapy is good and all but I'm still human. Bring on the drama. I'll go make popcorn while you pick."

Ruth scrolled through a few movies before settling on one and pressing pause until Sophie returned with the popcorn. A task that was taking far longer than the three minutes it should take to pop in the microwave. Ruth's phone lit up and her heart did a flip as she reached for it. Her heart sank again at the reply from Greta acknowledging Ruth's earlier message about staying in Sophie's. Ruth had messaged Ollie at the same time to check she got home okay, and Ollie had replied with one simple word.

Yes.

Sophie had advised Ruth to give Ollie a little space. To give her the night to cool off so Ollie didn't say anything reactive, or at least anything more than she already had. It was good advice, and Ruth should take it. But one more message wouldn't hurt, right? Sophie also said open communication was good, after all. Ruth typed out the words quickly before Sophie could return and snatch the phone from her hand.

I hope you're feeling okay. I'm here if you want to talk about anything. I know you'll be busy with Grace leaving tomorrow, but I'm around if you need help or photos of Piglet or well...anything.

Ruth almost signed off with three words that hadn't left her lips yet, but she didn't need Sophie's voice in her ear to know that it wasn't the time for that right now. She pressed send right as Sophie returned with the popcorn bowl and placed it between them.

"You were gone for a suspiciously long time and you're smiling weirdly. And you brought your phone with you. Are you going to tell me more about your mystery date, young lady?"

Sophie grabbed a handful of popcorn and nodded toward Ruth's phone where Ruth had placed it on the table in front of them during her interrogation of Sophie.

"Do you want me to question what you were doing on your phone, or do you want to press play so we can both avoid these conversations?"

Ruth grabbed the remote and fumbled with it as Sophie laughed while Ruth muttered under her breath, "Open communication my ass."

A couple hours later when Sophie shook her awake to head to bed, one solitary word from Ollie awaited her in reply.

Thanks.

❖

"Wait, hold up, Ruth is Roo? The Roo from that random drawing you always kept stuck to your wall?"

Olivia nodded as she piled scrambled eggs onto plates for them both and joined Grace at the table.

"Yup. The very same."

"Wow. Small world doesn't cut it for Ireland, does it?" Grace said with an incredulous look. "So, you're basically like childhood sweethearts with this epic beginning to a love story that you're royally screwing up by playing the silent treatment game."

Olivia glared at Grace as she chewed and swallowed the scrambled egg before replying. "I'm not playing games and I hate that implication. I replied, and I chose my words carefully."

"Word. Your word carefully. Seriously, one-word responses may as well be the silent treatment. What's your deal?" Grace said.

Olivia knew Grace had a point, but how could she describe what she was feeling, without delving too much into the epic emotional trainwreck her mind had ventured to on the previous day? The last thing she wanted was to drag up more of the past and her own issues for Grace, especially considering the less than steady decline Henry was on right now.

"I'm dealing with a lot right now and I'm trying to make sure I don't pile that on Ruth. I reacted badly to something she said when I dropped her off and I don't want to risk that happening again. I really like her, and she doesn't deserve to deal with all of that right now. She's going through enough, sorting through her own childhood issues."

Grace tilted her head and narrowed her eyes sceptically.

"Don't you think she should be involved in the decision of what she deserves a chance to deal with? You do realize healthy relationships aren't two perfect humans with zero baggage living happily ever after, right?"

Olivia would ordinarily scoff at relationship advice from her little sister. But the time they'd spent together over the past few weeks had made it clear to her that Grace wasn't so little anymore. She happened to make some valid points.

"I get that. But we're just starting out and getting to know each other. Now Ruth is dealing with new, maybe disappointing information about her parents. Throwing that into the mix with my parental issues while my father is actually dying, isn't it a bit too much, too soon?"

Grace looked at Olivia for long enough that the scrutiny made Olivia squirm in her seat.

"You're so full of bullshit I'm worried you're starting to believe it yourself, Livvie."

Olivia's mouth opened in shock and Grace laughed.

"Well, seriously. You're inventing reasons to push Ruth away because you actually care about her and that terrifies you. The fact is, those things aren't being *thrown* into the mix, they were already in the mix and you both dealt with them. You've been dealing with them, together. Like couples do. But you're not used to someone wanting to help you, you're used to being the one to help. And now you're paralyzed in fear, afraid that if you do let her help, she'll leave, and if you don't, well… she'll leave. So how about you go upstairs and deal with your daddy issues before you let it fuck up every future relationship you have?"

Olivia's mouth opened and closed a few times as Grace shrugged her shoulders and continued eating her breakfast.

"You're mean," Olivia eventually grumbled in reply.

"No, I'm just sick of seeing my big sister self-sabotage. I get that you don't want to feel obliged to make things up with Dad, and that's your choice. I'm never going to pretend I fully understand what it was like for you, because I never had to, you made sure of that. You took care of me, you still do. So how about taking care of yourself now and doing it for you?"

Olivia gulped back the lump in her throat and sighed.

"He's very sick. I don't want to go in there and drag stuff up and upset him, upsetting you in return. I may not have the same relationship with him as you do, but I'm not heartless. I don't want to hurt him for the sake of it."

Grace reached out and covered Olivia's hand with hers.

"He's already hurting, Liv. However the conversation goes, it'll give him far more closure than feeling like you're a stranger. I promise that you can't say anything to him that he hasn't said to himself many times over. But this needs to be about you."

Grace pulled her up and enveloped her in a tight hug. Olivia held on a little longer than usual. If there was one thing she would forever be grateful to her parents for, it was Grace.

"I've got a couple of things to do before I grab the train, so I'm going to head out now. Promise you'll call me if anything changes?" Grace said.

The house had an eerie silence to it after Grace was gone, and Olivia sat willing herself to move. Her phone lit up and she grabbed at the distraction to delay her actions for another few moments. She opened the message from Ruth to an adorable photo of Piglet followed by a message.

Piglet demanded I show you this. No need to reply, I know you've got a lot to deal with, but I'm thinking of you. That part was from me, not Piglet.

Olivia's smile turned into a chuckle at the second message that popped up.

Piglet's probably thinking of you, too. She's a hard one to read sometimes.

Olivia started to type a reply when the alarm they had installed next to Henry's bed for emergencies started to ring, sending a notification to her phone, too. Olivia's heart dropped. In the weeks since she had arrived, Henry had stubbornly refused to ever use the bell, even when he shouldn't have been walking around alone. It would take a lot to make him press it, so Olivia dropped her phone and ran toward the room.

She sprinted through the bedroom door and saw Henry struggling to catch his breath. The fear in his bulging eyes stopped her momentarily in her tracks. She moved quickly, pulling his oxygen mask toward him, and holding it to his face to lower the pressure on his lungs. She took some deep breaths herself as he did the same and his hand dropped to cover hers over the mask.

Olivia's heart was beating rapidly, and it pounded in her ears. She was a nurse. Medical emergencies weren't scary to her. Seeing someone struggle to breathe was a daily occurrence. But that wasn't what caused the racing adrenaline that still coursed through her body and created this tightening in her chest. As she glanced down to see Henry staring at her, the fear now turning to exhaustion in his eyes, she knew it had nothing to do with that at all.

The fear that neared desperation now was caused by the stark realisation that this could've been it. The sand running out of the timer, the inevitable end to chances Olivia hadn't even thought she wanted. But it was clear to her now that she did. Not because of Ruth, not because of Grace. Not even because of the soft grip of her father's hand around her wrist.

This was about her. She wanted this chance for herself, and she deserved to take it before it was gone.

"You need to do this *one* damn thing for me and stay alive just a little longer, Dad. I'm begging you not to take this from me. I know you're ready, but I'm not. Do you hear me? I'm not ready."

CHAPTER SIXTEEN

Ruth hovered for a moment next to the bag she had set down after knocking tentatively on the oak door. She was worried the knock hadn't been loud enough and the food would go to waste outside, but knocking again felt too intrusive, if the first had been louder than she thought. There was the doorbell option, but if Henry was sleeping, she didn't want to disturb him.

Sometimes Ruth wondered if everyone else spent such a significant portion of their days overthinking these inconsequential actions. She eventually settled on knocking once more before she turned to walk briskly down the path.

"Ruth?"

She had been so focused on making it down the driveway that she hadn't heard the soft click of the door opening. Ollie's voice made her stop in her tracks, and her heart picked up pace. Ruth had been prepared for this, of course. If you knocked on the door of the house someone was living in there was a fair chance they'd answer. Especially if you knocked twice. The part of her that worried she was bordering on stalking had her rooted to the spot, while the part that longed to lay eyes on Ollie again was secretly cheering.

"Hey, sorry, I just wanted to drop those off. I didn't mean to disturb you."

Ruth turned and spoke the words quickly from where she stood. Ollie looked at her quizzically before her eyes dropped to the bag Ruth had left behind. Ollie's face lit up at the clear outline of the item Ruth had strategically placed on top in the hopes of this exact reaction. She couldn't help laughing as Ollie snatched it up right away and inhaled the scent of the freshly baked muffin.

"It's never a disturbance if it includes these," Ollie said.

"Good to know," Ruth replied with a smile.

They stood in silence for a moment and Ruth shifted her feet awkwardly. She should move, either toward Ollie or toward the gate, but she stood in between, unable to decide.

"I'm sorry I haven't messaged much. Things have just…" Ollie trailed off with a shrug.

Ruth had heard from a few people now that Henry had declined even further in the week since they had returned from Ollie's mom's. Although Ruth's anxiety did its best to convince her that Ollie was avoiding her specifically and she should take the hint, her heart told her otherwise. Standing here looking at the varied emotions playing across Ollie's face, Ruth knew her heart was right.

"Don't worry about that. I just wanted you to know I'm thinking about you and that I'm here. And that good things like muffins still exist, so it's not all bad." Ruth took a few steps toward Ollie as she spoke and was encouraged by the small smile that graced Ollie's lips.

"Definitely not all bad. Thank you for the reminder." Ollie's eyes met Ruth's, and Ruth's heart pounded as they stared at one another. Her body screamed for her to move a little closer so she could reach out and touch Ollie. A graze of her fingertips along Ollie's arm, a soft touch against her cheek, any contact would do. Ollie glanced behind her, and the moment passed as Ruth gulped back the rising emotions.

"Anyway, I should go. There's enough in there to keep you going for a couple of days," Ruth said.

The door pulled open wider, and Grace popped up behind Ollie with a big smile plastered across her face.

"Ruth! What are you doing standing out here like a stranger? Come in."

Grace looked at Ollie and tutted as she added, "Where'd your manners go?"

Ollie's face flamed red and Ruth bit her lip. Spending more time with Ollie was always a bonus, but she wanted that to be on Ollie's terms.

"No, honestly, I was just dropping stuff off," Ruth said.

She flicked her eyes to Ollie again, trying to convey to her that it was okay. Grace huffed and picked the bag up from the floor.

"Your girlfriend brought us food and you have her standing on the step? Seriously, you suck. I'm going to put up the kettle so we can make tea and eat this stuff. *All* of us." That last part was said with a pointed look between Ollie and Ruth. Grace turned on her heel then and walked away, leaving Ollie and Ruth standing even more awkwardly than before. *Girlfriend.* That's what they were to each other still, right? That meant something more than hovering in silence.

"I understand if you need more time, I can go, and you can tell Grace I had plans. But I'm glad to see you. I've missed you," Ruth said.

"I've missed you, too. Come in, please. I should've said it from the start. I was just so focused on you being here that I didn't remember I could actually ask you to stay. Plus, I know my dad would love to see you, too."

My dad. It sounded so casual from Ollie's lips that it startled Ruth, but she didn't want to draw attention to it. She smiled softly and followed Ollie through to the kitchen where

Grace was setting three cups of tea on the table and pulling some of the food from the bag.

"Glad you both saw a little sense. Dad's still sleeping, but he'll love this when he wakes," Grace said as she set aside one of the pastries.

"Sophie mentioned they were his favourite when I was picking stuff up. Oh, and she put the chocolate swirls in for you, too."

If Ruth didn't know better, she could've sworn Grace's cheeks pinked a little at that. *Interesting.* Funny how the reaction was remarkably similar to Sophie's as she had packed the stuff up for Ruth earlier. Seemed like maybe, just maybe, Sophie's mystery date might be solved. Ruth wondered if Ollie was aware her sister was dating Ruth's best friend.

"That was sweet of her," Ollie said with an oblivious smile. *Guess not.*

"I thought you'd be in college until tomorrow, but Sophie insisted I bring them anyway to save for you," Ruth said.

She was pretty sure Sophie had known exactly where Grace was and hadn't wanted to be caught out as to why she held that information.

"Livvie called me yesterday. Dad took a bit of a turn, so it seemed best for me to be close," Grace said with a solemn tone.

Ruth nodded. She wasn't sure what to say that would bring any comfort to the situation. Nothing was particularly comforting about the current reality.

"I'm trying to convince Liv she can still go to her best friend's wedding this weekend, but she's stubbornly refusing," Grace said.

"I'm not going to the city a couple hours' drive away from you and Dad when we both felt it necessary for you to come home from college early."

There it was again—dad. Something had shifted since Ruth last saw Ollie, and by the soft smile on Grace's lips at Ollie's words, Ruth knew it was a positive change.

"Huh, what wedding? I'm actually photographing a wedding in the city this weekend. I'm heading up there later today to get prepared," Ruth said.

Ruth had met the two women at a pride event before she moved back from the city, and they'd booked her on the spot after seeing her work displayed. They were a beautiful couple, and Ruth was excited to be a part of the day.

"My friend Dani is *finally* marrying the love of her life, Ruby. They had a whole on-again, off-again thing the past few years when timing never seemed to align, so I'm excited they are finally getting their happily-ever-after. I'm sorry to be missing it. Especially if you'll be there." Ollie looked up at Ruth with a soft, sad smile.

"Yep, it's the same wedding. I'll be sure to give you a sneak preview of the photos when I'm back. But if anything happens while I'm away, will you call me? I want to be here for you," Ruth said.

Ollie nodded, and Ruth caught her eye, trying her best to convey the sincerity of her words.

"That's bizarre. It really is a small world, isn't it?"

Grace snapped them out of it and Ruth smiled at her.

"It is. I know it's a small county, but me living in the same village as your dad, and now me photographing your best friend's wedding, it's definitely bizarre," Ruth said.

"Not to mention the fact that you both knew each other twenty years before any of that even happened. Like what are the chances you'd meet online, too, after all of that," Grace said with a chuckle.

Ruth frowned as she tried to understand Grace's words.

"I'm sorry, I'm confused. Me and Ollie?" Ruth was sure

she must have misunderstood until she looked at Ollie's face, which had drained of colour. Ollie gave her a sheepish smile and shrugged.

"Sorry, I know it's weird to hear this way. But I figured it out when we were at Nora's house and I saw the photo of you," Ollie said.

Ruth's head was spinning, and Ollie's words were like an anagram she didn't have the code to crack.

"Nora's? What are you talking about?" Ruth asked.

Grace glanced back and forth between them and then got up from the table, grabbing their cups.

"I'm going to go tidy." She mouthed *sorry* at Ollie before she left, and Ollie turned fully toward Ruth.

"It's just this weird coincidence. I was in the hospital with you. I mean, Grace was the one actually in the hospital, but I was visiting while you were in after…"

After the fire, Ruth finished the sentence in her head. A lot of those memories were still jumbled, but some things had always stood out. One of which was niggling at her mind as pieces started to form together.

"Livvie," Ruth whispered.

Olivia nodded, her eyes brightening at the word.

"I didn't know if you'd remember. Or if it would be too hard for you to remember that time. I meant to tell you but—"

"But what?" Ruth said as it hit her that Ollie had said she'd known this since Nora's house.

"You had a lot of information already thrown at you that day, and although this part wasn't a bad thing, I didn't want to add to it. Especially since you weren't in a great place when I came to the car. I wanted to protect you."

Ollie had said the worst possible thing without even knowing it. Ruth's stomach dropped and anger rose up at the words. It was another part of her past that someone close to her had decided Ruth was too fragile to know. Ruth stood quickly, needing to get out of there before she unleashed it all on Ollie in a way that Ollie didn't deserve. But with all the unresolved stuff still swimming around her head about Greta, it felt like another person seeing Ruth as weak and vulnerable.

"Where are you going? I was going to tell you."

"When?" Ruth shot out the word before she could stop herself, as the anger she had yet to process started to spill over. "Because if your sister hadn't said anything, I would still be oblivious to yet another part of my past. When would you have deemed me competent enough to handle this?"

Ollie pulled back as if she had been slapped and Ruth clenched her fists at her sides, taking some deep breaths to calm the pounding of her heart.

"You're angry. About more than just this, I'm guessing. Do you want to sit and calm for a minute so we can talk?" Ollie asked.

"I am so damn sick of everyone treating me with kid gloves." Ruth took another couple of inhales and shook herself. "I'm going to go. Because I know myself well enough to know what I can handle, and how to manage with things I can't. You're dealing with a lot right now, and I'm going to go handle this like I've been doing for years. Bye, Ollie."

At that, Ruth turned and walked out of the house, not letting the tears fall until she was safely past the gate and out of eyesight, unwilling to allow Ollie to believe her point was proven by Ruth's overflowing emotions.

❖

Did that really happen?

Olivia started at the closed door, still trying to catch up with the shift in the day. She had been so happy to see Ruth outside, and throughout their conversation things started to feel somewhat normal again. The look of hurt on Ruth's face, by something that Olivia thought would eventually be a nice memory for them to share, flashed through her mind.

"I am so sorry. I put my foot in it big time." Grace walked out and looked at her apologetically.

"It's okay. I should've told her before you did, anyway," Ollie said.

"Seemed like a little bit of an overreaction though, no?" Grace asked.

Olivia understood why it would seem that way, but given the other things Ruth was still holding inside, Olivia knew exactly where the reaction stemmed from.

"She's found out quite a bit lately that her aunt had kept from her, most likely out of a sense of protection. It's a sore spot for her."

More like a gaping wound that Olivia had poked wide open.

"Anyway, I need to get Dad's meds. I'll bring him the pastry, too," Olivia said.

Grace smiled softly at her, and Olivia furrowed her brow. "What?"

"It's just nice to hear you call him that is all. I know things still aren't perfect between you two, but seeing the change in you both since I got back has been good. It makes me happy."

Olivia nodded and grabbed the pastry from the counter-top.

"I know it does, but that's not why I did it. When I thought he was almost gone the other day, I just realized I was punishing myself more than anyone by holding on to everything so tightly. I needed to let it go, and to do that I needed to see him for who he is now."

"I'm proud of you, Livvie," Grace said. She gave her a one-armed squeeze before Olivia walked toward their father's room.

There hadn't been a big, emotional heart-to-heart between her and Henry. That was part of what had held Olivia back from moving on for so long. She didn't want to dredge through the past with someone who was so far from the person she remembered. Sitting with her father after the scare they had, she realized she didn't have to. There was no manual to this, and nobody got to dictate what healing looked like for her or their relationship. Olivia didn't need to write up a list of his mistakes and forgive each one. But something shifted that day between them, and within Olivia, too.

"Ruth dropped off some pastries. You up for a little?" Olivia asked as she set the plate on the pull-out table beside her father's bed while she gathered his medication.

"Not right now, Livvie. I'm glad Ruth is around again. She's a good girl."

Olivia's eyes prickled with tears that had been far too close to the surface lately.

"Hey, little Livvie, what's wrong?" Henry's words were raspy, and he reached a shaking hand out to grasp Olivia's wrist. She turned toward him as the dam burst and tears fell down her face.

"Come here, my girl," Henry said, and Olivia didn't resist this time. She let him pull her down onto the bed and she curled against his chest. She sobbed in a way she hadn't remembered doing in a long time.

"Shh, it's okay. I've got you."

Her father's soft, soothing words surrounded her as the tears flowed slower now. Lying in his arms was such a foreign, yet familiar feeling. Like a memory she hadn't quite allowed herself to recall until now. The notes of a softly whistled tune met her ears and Olivia smiled.

"Hey, what's going on in here without me?"

Grace walked through the door and Olivia lifted her gaze but didn't move from her spot beside their dad.

"Hop up, then," Henry said, and Grace did just that.

He kept up the soft whistles as Grace reached a hand across and gripped Olivia's. She looked over her father's chest that rose and fell with each breath and glanced at her sister. Grace's cheeks were wet with her own tears and Olivia found the sight comforting rather than upsetting. It was a sad time, but they were here, together, and that filled Olivia with far more peace than sadness.

She must have drifted off to sleep at some point, exhausted from the week. Before Olivia even opened her eyes, she registered the stillness beside her. She blinked and looked over at Grace lying across from her still asleep. Her father's chest no longer rose and fell the way it had before they drifted off. Her initial instinct was to jump up and do everything she could to make him breathe again. But that wouldn't work, and even if it did, it wasn't what he would want.

Her father had got to slip away quietly with his two daughters sleeping peacefully in his arms, and she wouldn't take that from him. Because if the past few days had shown her anything, when she finally allowed herself to see it, it was that this was exactly what her dad was holding on for. Olivia wished she could let Grace sleep so she wouldn't have to witness the crumpling of her face when she woke and realized he was gone. She wished more than anything that she could shield Grace from the pain.

But that wasn't her job now. Grace didn't need protecting. She needed her sister by her side to walk with her through the grief. Olivia was grateful she got to be here for this, and even more grateful she'd allowed herself to experience the full array of feelings it brought without having to shut any out. Sadness, grief, fear, gratitude, so many swirling emotions. But one stood out ahead of all the rest, and that's what she would hold on to, above all else.

Love.

CHAPTER SEVENTEEN

"The wedding was beautiful. Seriously, they both looked amazing. I can't wait to show them their photos. I got some magical shots if I do say so myself."

Ruth had gotten off the train from the city and stopped by the café to grab a coffee before heading home. It was finally time she had a face-to-face chat with Greta, who had been avoiding Ruth this past week just as much as Ruth had been avoiding her.

"You brag as much as you want, lady. You know I'm the biggest fan of your work," Sophie said as she passed over a to-go cup.

Ruth lifted the cup to her lips and took a sip, savouring the sweet addition of the caramel flavouring on today's special.

"Have you spoken to Ollie?" Sophie's tone lowered at the words and Ruth sighed, disappointed that her answer wasn't a good one.

"Nope. I know I'm the one who stormed out and all, but I sent her a photo of Dani and Ruby with their permission and radio silence. I expected at least a reaction to that, you know?"

Sophie frowned and Ruth tilted her head, wondering what she wasn't saying.

"You didn't hear?" Sophie asked.

Ruth's stomach dropped and her chest squeezed tightly. No, she hadn't heard a thing, and only one thing could have Sophie looking so devastated.

"No. When?" It was all Ruth could manage to choke out.

"The day you left. I'm sorry, I figured Greta would've told you," Sophie said.

"No, once again she did not. Why didn't you? We were texting just yesterday." Ruth tried to rein in her anger, knowing Sophie hadn't done anything wrong here.

"I thought you knew, and I didn't want to throw you off while you were at the wedding yesterday by bringing it up. If Greta hadn't told you I was sure Ollie would have," Sophie said.

"No, nobody did. I asked Ollie to call me if he passed, and she said she would. I wanted to be there for her."

Ruth's feelings around Mr B. passing were such a mixed bag. Her own emotions were one part, having known him for fifteen years filled with positive memories. But that was compounded by the fact that he was Ollie's father, and Ruth's feelings for Ollie. Regardless, she would've expected at the least a text from Ollie to let her know. It wasn't about her at the moment, but she couldn't stop the hurt that surfaced all the same.

"The funeral's tomorrow, so you can be there for her then," Sophie said with a sympathetic look.

Ruth nodded and took her coffee. She walked back to the cottage with a mind full of varying scenarios playing out. She would go to the funeral, of course. For Mr B., and for Ollie. Even if Ollie didn't want her support, Ruth would be there. Ruth walked through the front door of the cottage and set down her bag as Greta rounded the corner from the living room.

"I'm glad you're back, honey. I have some bad news," Greta said with a sorrowful look on her face.

"What, that Mr B. died, or that my parents probably wouldn't have accepted me? Or is there some other thing you're keeping from me to protect me?" The words spilled out of Ruth before she could stop them and Greta blinked, looking at her for a moment.

"Let's go sit and talk," Greta said finally, making her way back into the living room. Ruth followed silently and sat across from her aunt.

"He died days ago, and you didn't tell me," Ruth said softly.

"I know. But you were working, and I didn't like the idea of you all alone finding out about that. Whether you like it or not, Roo, my job is to protect you, and has been for a long time. That doesn't switch off the minute you turn eighteen."

Ruth nodded at the truth in Greta's words. That's what she wanted right? The truth. And it was time she asked for it.

"Why didn't you tell me your parents kicked you out? And my mom didn't help you either, all because you're gay? Would she have hated me, too?"

Tears started to flow fast and freely down Ruth's cheeks as Greta moved toward her and placed a hand over Ruth's.

"Oh no, honey. You've got it wrong," Greta said as she stroked Ruth's arm softly.

"Don't lie to me. I went to my childhood home, which was yours, too, I guess. I met a neighbour there, Nora. She told me what happened. That's why you don't talk about them, isn't it? It's why you never tell me anything. You're trying to protect me, but it hurts."

"It wasn't about protecting you, Ruth. I was protecting myself."

Ruth's head shot up at that and she stared at Greta who was staring right back at her, not a hint of secrecy on her face.

"Yes, my parents kicked me out. But none of that was Kate's fault."

"But you didn't speak to each other after it. She didn't have your back," Ruth whispered. She half hoped it wasn't true and that her mom had come to Greta's defence. But then, why wouldn't Ruth have known her aunt before they died?

"No, she didn't. Not at first anyway. But you're seeing things through the lens you have now, not the way it was then. We were young. I could barely stand up for myself, and I'd had time to come to terms with it. Kate was shocked. You've grown up in a community that never made you feel wrong for being who you are. We grew up in a house that wasn't all that welcoming of difference. Expecting your mother, who was a teenager at the time, to automatically know how to be an ally to me without any preparation or guidance was too much. She needed time, and I didn't give it to her. And then, well, it ran out."

Greta's eyes dropped and she sighed heavily.

"I left and I didn't look back. Your mom wrote to me after I moved here. I'm still not even sure how she got my address, but I ignored it. It was too hard. I figured when I dealt with my own feelings around it, I would reach out and open the lines of communication again. After our parents passed away and were out of the picture, I kept trying to get myself to do it. But I was terrified Kate wouldn't accept me and then I'd lose her all over again. Then when the hospital called and told me… well, it was too late."

Ruth covered Greta's hand with hers and squeezed softly.

"I'm sorry. It's been hard thinking I had this idea of who my parents were and then now not knowing if they would even like who I am. I shouldn't have jumped down your throat like that, though," Ruth said.

"Of course they would like who you are, Ruth. You are the best thing I've ever done with my life, and I'm absolutely certain your parents felt the same."

"But you said yourself you were afraid my mom wouldn't accept you. How can you be so sure now? You can't ask her."

Greta raised an eyebrow and looked at her as if the answer was obvious.

"*You*, sweetheart. You are my proof. Your mom entrusted me with the most important part of her life. The hospital didn't call me at random to come and take you. Yes, I was the next of kin. But the only way they could have known that was from your parents. They chose me, Roo. They chose me to care for you. That's how I know."

How had Ruth never considered that fact? She laughed a little and Greta smiled in return as they embraced. Her parents would never have chosen Greta to raise her if they didn't agree with who she was. Or with who Ruth turned out to be, too.

"Thank you. For everything. I want you to know how grateful I am to have the life I've had with you. I miss my parents, but you've made sure I could miss them happily, in safety and comfort. I love you."

Greta kissed the top of Ruth's head and dried her eyes.

"I love you, too, Roo. Now let's have some lunch and you can tell me about the mess you've gotten yourself into with Henry's girl."

❖

Olivia couldn't believe the number of people that showed up to her father's funeral. It was at least the whole village if not more, and she was grateful for the kind words everyone had spoken and the memories they shared. She spotted Ruth during the ceremony, too, standing with Greta. Every time Olivia looked their way, which happened to be quite a lot, Ruth was watching her. Olivia longed to walk toward her and beg for them to forget all the ridiculous things that had kept them apart for too long. Things that were a waste of the precious time they had.

A surprising turn of events was seeing Grace comforted by none other than Sophie, in a far more than friendly manner. Although the surprise seemed to be solely on her part when nobody else batted an eye. Olivia had to admit they made a cute couple. They sat close together at the same table as Olivia in the community centre. It had been filled with chairs, tables, and a buffet of more food than Olivia could believe. The village had all pitched in to bring the many trays and dishes in celebration of her father's life.

Olivia was warmed and grateful. She finally understood the draw to the tight knit community and the residents whose hearts were as big as their mouths sometimes were. Speaking of which, Mrs Guiney picked that moment to slide into the chair next to Olivia and place a soft hand on her arm.

"Your dad talked about you all the time. He was always so proud of his Livvie. I'm glad you were there with him when…"

Mrs Guiney trailed off as her voice choked and Olivia smiled softly.

"I am, too. And from what I've heard, I believe I have you to thank for organising everything here today. It really means a lot," Olivia replied.

"We take care of each other here, dear. I hope you stick around long enough to see more of it."

Mrs Guiney got up and left as Olivia sat wondering if

she hoped the same. Her dad was gone now, and once she had his house cleaned up with Grace, what reason did she have to stay? Her eyes landed on Ruth then, who was standing in the corner talking to Greta and another woman whom Olivia didn't know. Ruth's eyes flicked to hers and stayed there for a beat before returning to the conversation.

"I think I'm going to take a walk," Olivia said to Grace as she stood.

"Do you want me to go with you?" Grace asked, concern etched into her features.

"No, Gracie. I am capable of taking a walk by myself. Just stay and make more gooey eyes at your girlfriend." Olivia threw in a wink and Grace shrugged, unashamed. As she should be.

Olivia caught Ruth's eye again before she walked out the door. She hoped the footsteps that followed her were Ruth's, and she wasn't disappointed.

"Ollie?" Ruth asked softly as she walked up behind her.

"Hey. I was just going to take a walk, get some air." Olivia turned and waited for Ruth to reach her.

"Mind some company?" Ruth asked hesitantly.

"Well, I'd probably get lost without my tour guide."

Olivia's heart leapt at Ruth's smile as they walked side by side in no particular direction.

"It was a lovely service. Grace's words made me cry," Ruth said.

"Me too. She did great. Everyone made it really special."

"You didn't call me," Ruth blurted out.

Olivia paused for a moment but then kept walking, trying to figure out how to respond.

"You were upset when you left that day, and it all happened pretty suddenly. I thought about calling you. I typed out a lot of messages. But I didn't know what to say. I figured Greta or Sophie would let you know, and well…I just didn't know what to say."

Olivia looked up and realized they had made their way to the river that Ruth loved. They walked toward the riverbank, and she sat down as Ruth joined her.

"I told you to call me if anything changed. I wanted to be there for you," Ruth whispered, hurt evident in her voice.

"Yeah, but that was before…"

"Do you really think that would have mattered, Ollie? Your dad died. I don't care about what happened before. I would've been here," Ruth said.

Olivia was quiet for a moment. Words bubbled under the surface that she wasn't sure quite how to string together. Not in a way that anyone else could understand.

"That's just not how things have ever worked for me, okay? I'm the one who gets the calls. Someone needs help and I'm there. Not the other way around. I hurt you by making you feel like I was another person hiding things from you. I wanted to call you, but I knew if I did, I would crack. I would break down, and I don't get to do that because I'm the one who picks up everyone else's damn pieces. I don't get to break."

Olivia's voice proved her wrong on that last sentence as it broke around the words. Tears formed and fell quicker than she could stop them, and once the dam opened it wouldn't shut. Strong arms wrapped around her and held her tight as she sobbed against Ruth's chest. After a few minutes Ruth's fingers were under her chin and she lifted Olivia's face to meet hers. Ruth placed a soft kiss against Olivia's lips, and Olivia melted into the touch, wanting nothing more than to get lost in Ruth and forget everything else. Ruth pulled back too quickly, and Olivia whimpered as she stared right into her eyes.

"That shit ends now, do you understand? If you need to

break, you break. Because I am right here to pick up every beautiful piece of you, Olivia Bell. Please, let me."

Olivia nodded, and kissed Ruth more, as they wrapped their arms tight around each other. Right there as the ever-changing river flowed beside them.

CHAPTER EIGHTEEN

As Ollie unlocked the door to her house, Ruth sent a text to Sophie asking her to let Greta and Grace know that Ruth and Ollie were safe. As she shot off the message, Ollie turned her around and pulled her back into a deep, heated kiss. Ruth pulled back a little bit as she considered Ollie's vulnerable state.

"Are you sure you want this? I want to stay with you tonight, but it doesn't need to be anything more than being together. We could snuggle up and watch a movie or—"

Ollie cut her off with a finger over her lips as she pulled Ruth toward the stairs.

"I'm sure, darling. I appreciate the chivalry, but right now I want to get lost in you and I want you to get lost in me, too. Please?"

Ruth almost melted into a puddle on the spot, but instead she nodded enthusiastically and followed Ollie up the stairs to her bedroom.

They undressed each other slowly, taking their time to unravel every layer separating their bodies. Ruth kissed each inch of Ollie as she revealed it and was bolstered by the soft moans coming from Ollie where she stood. Ruth dropped to her knees as she slipped the final piece of clothing, Ollie's underwear, off and deposited it to the floor. She looked up to find Ollie looking down at her and taking in the scene with an undiluted longing in her eyes.

Ruth was grateful to already be kneeling. She was sure her legs would have given way at the sight. She ran her hands up and down Ollie's thighs and parted them with a firm press as Ollie gulped. Ruth bit her bottom lip as she ran a finger between Ollie's folds and her mouth watered at the glistening that already awaited her.

"Are you gonna just stare at it all day or—"

Ollie's word cut off on a moan as Ruth pressed a finger inside her.

"Sorry, what was that?" Ruth asked.

"Fuck. Nothing. Don't stop," Ollie replied.

Ruth pressed a second finger inside as she stroked in a slow and steady rhythm, keeping her eyes on Ollie's face above her. She moved her lips forward and placed soft kisses up Ollie's thighs as they parted even more for her. Ruth ran her tongue over Ollie's core and hummed in appreciation.

"You taste so damn good," Ruth said as she pulled back to take in the desperation on Ollie's face.

"I don't know if I can stand for this," Ollie murmured as she reached behind her and found nothing to grip. Ruth smiled and pulled her fingers from the warmth and nudged Ollie's hip until she turned. Ollie whimpered in response to the loss of contact.

"If you bend over you can grip that bed right there," Ruth said with a salacious lilt to her tone.

The heat between her own legs amplified when Ollie complied with her suggestion. Seeing Ollie bent over and exposed to her, so vulnerable and so damn beautiful, made it impossible for Ruth to draw this out any longer. She ran her hands over Ollie's ass before moving to grip her hips. Ruth ran her tongue slowly back and forth over Ollie's centre before pushing it inside Ollie's warmth.

Ruth dug her fingers into Ollie's skin and curled her tongue after several strokes, alternating between both until Ollie's legs began to shake. She kept her tongue there to taste every drop of sweetness as Ollie orgasmed in a loud cry. Ollie turned to sit on the bed and tugged at Ruth's arm to pull her up. Ruth obliged and straddled Ollie's lap to kiss her deeply. Ollie pressed a hand to Ruth's ass, lifting her gently as she slid her other hand between them. She pressed two fingers easily inside Ruth and palmed her clit in circular motions. Ruth moved her hips in tandem with Ollie's fingers as they continued to explore each other's mouths.

"Fuck, Ollie," Ruth hissed as she threw her head back when Ollie added a third finger. Ollie wrapped her lips around Ruth's hardened nipple and sucked as Ruth clenched around her fingers. Tidal waves of pleasure coursed through her as Ollie held a steady arm around her back so she could let go. She panted loudly as the last of the waves ebbed and Ollie pulled her back up to meet her lips once more.

They moved almost in tandem until they were lying on their sides face-to-face with limbs intertwined. They kissed with a slow intensity, as if the melding of their mouths could pour out all the unsaid words between them. Ollie pulled back and brushed a strand of hair from Ruth's face. She continued the gentle stroke of her fingers down Ruth's cheek as they got lost in each other's eyes.

"You're extraordinarily beautiful, you know that?" Ollie whispered softly.

"Mmm, you're not so bad yourself," Ruth replied, sneaking another kiss in between words.

"I saw your mom at the service," Ruth said. "Did everything go okay there?"

Ollie nodded as she moved her fingers to trace up and down Ruth's back.

"She didn't stay after the funeral, which I was glad for. And she was on her best behaviour. She offered to stay close and help us sort through stuff over the next few days, but I think that's something that we'll do better without her. I promised to visit soon, which helped."

"How do you feel about visiting? And sorting the house? We don't need to talk if you don't want to, but I'm here if you do," Ruth asked.

"I like talking to you," Ollie said. Her tone sounded as if it was a surprise.

"I should hope so," Ruth replied with a grin, noting to herself how comfortable she was lying there in Ollie's arms, content to talk about anything and everything.

"Well, I mean, even about stuff I don't usually like discussing. I still want to talk to you, which isn't usual for me. You make me feel like I can."

Ruth's stomach flipped at the words, and she placed another lingering kiss on Ollie's lips.

"I'm glad. Because you can, always. I want to hear everything there is to know about you Ollie. Even the parts that make your brow furrow and your hands clench," Ruth said with raised eyebrows.

Ollie laughed and tightened her grip on Ruth's back. She used the knee that was already placed between Ruth's legs to apply more pressure, and Ruth gasped. Ollie leaned in to kiss her way from the nape of Ruth's neck up to her earlobe. She sucked the soft lobe gently before whispering, "This is definitely not an avoidance tactic. So, if I promise to do all the talking you want later, can we pause for me to devour your gorgeous body first?"

Ruth gulped and nodded. No further words needed, as her body readily accepted the offer.

❖

Olivia walked into the kitchen the next morning to make them breakfast as Ruth hopped in for a quick shower. Or, more accurately, as Ruth continued the shower Olivia had started before they got distracted beneath the water together.

"Hey, sleepyhead, I was going to offer you breakfast but I didn't know if you and Ruth would be staying in your love nest for the day. There's still enough mix for a couple omelettes, though, if you want to throw them on."

Grace walked toward Olivia as she spoke and pulled her in for a tight hug. It was something she had been doing often over the past few days. Olivia hugged her back and spotted Sophie already sitting at the table cutting up her own omelette.

"Thanks, I'll do that. You two get on okay after we left yesterday?" Olivia asked, as she went about pouring the eggs into the still warm frying pan.

"Yeah, we stayed late enough to see Mr O' Reilley pull out his guitar and the singsong got underway. I was going to stay at Sophie's, but I was worried in case Ruth didn't stay and you'd be alone." Grace gave her a sly grin as she added, "Clearly no fear of that though, eh?"

Heat crept up Olivia's neck and she admonished herself. Grace was sitting at the table having breakfast with the girlfriend Olivia didn't even know she had until yesterday, so she did not get the upper hand here.

"No fear of it for you either. Mind telling me when this all began? I feel like the fact that you've been dating my girlfriend's best friend is relevant information," Olivia said.

"Technically, I was seeing Sophie before I even knew about you and Ruth, so *you* began dating *my* girlfriend's best friend," Grace shot back with a smug smile.

"Hold up. You've been dating for that long and decided to say nothing? How did you even get away with that in this village?" Olivia asked incredulously.

"Because you don't actually interact with anyone in the village, bar Ruth, so it wasn't like you'd have found out from Mrs Guiney, who you practically ran out of our house," Grace scoffed. Ruth walked in just as Olivia flipped the omelettes onto the waiting plates.

"She deserved it," Olivia grumbled. She set a plate in front of Ruth and sat across from her.

"Why didn't you tell me?" Olivia directed her question at Ruth, who seemed to be unfazed by the fact that Sophie and Grace were here together.

"It wasn't my thing to tell. Plus, I didn't suspect until the day I brought the pastries here. Clearly, I've been a little preoccupied and out of the loop," Ruth replied.

They gazed at each other before Sophie cleared her throat and pointed a fork between them.

"So did you two finally work your shit out?" Sophie asked.

Olivia admired the bluntness of the question even if it had Ruth rolling her eyes at her friend.

"Yes, we did. Not that it's any of your business," Ruth shot back with a huff.

"Oh, it's definitely my business when you're moping on my couch eating ice cream over what were clearly very fixable problems. I was this close to knocking your heads together."

Sophie held her thumb and forefinger close together to emphasize her point and Olivia laughed at Ruth's reddened cheeks.

"You don't get to judge when you decide to keep your

romance a secret. What's up there?" Ruth asked, glancing between Sophie and Grace.

"Well, we weren't keeping it a secret exactly. But you were both so damn skittish about relationships in general, we were not about to give you any reason to use this as an excuse as to why you two wouldn't work out. Plus, sneaking around was kind of a little fun for a while. But being able to do double dates is way more fun," Grace said as she wagged her eyebrows.

They talked more over breakfast and then they all moved to the living room to watch crappy television and chill in their pyjamas for the rest of the morning. Olivia sat with Ruth's head in her lap, lazily stroking her hair as they took turns telling stories about Olivia's father. Some of which had them laughing and some crying. Olivia found that the stories didn't bring any resentment or even jealousy about the time she missed with him. Instead, she was filled with gratitude to have time to learn so much more about him from each of the women surrounding her.

Olivia and Grace had a meeting with their father's solicitor later in the day to discuss the will and finalize any outstanding paperwork. She would then spend the week with Grace sorting through the house that had been her father's home for the past fifteen years. A place filled with memories that Olivia still had so much to learn about. The thought didn't terrify her as much as it did the first time she pulled into the driveway outside.

"I can bring up boxes from the café tomorrow, we have plenty of packaging stuff from our online orders, so that'll help get things organized," Sophie said as she and Ruth got ready to head home before Grace and Olivia left for the solicitors. A lump formed in Olivia's throat as the four of them stood near the door saying their goodbyes. The meeting would be difficult, and sorting through the stuff would surely surface emotions Olivia wasn't totally prepared for. But right now, for once, she didn't have to deal with it alone.

"Call me after the meeting. I mean it this time," Ruth whispered as she kissed Olivia softly.

"I will, I promise." *I love you.* Olivia added the last part in her head as the truth of the words surged through her so clearly in that moment. She wanted to say those words to Ruth, but she wanted them alone when she said them for the first time. Looking into Ruth's eyes before closing the door behind them, Olivia had no doubt that Ruth felt the same. They loved each other, and whatever happened this week or beyond, that was all the comfort Olivia needed in the world.

CHAPTER NINETEEN

S o, you're moving to Wicker Hill?" Ruth asked Grace as they sat with Sophie to pack up the pile of stuff to give away. Ollie had gone out to grab dinner for them all while they worked. They had made good progress already on sorting most of the stuff into piles for either charity, the attic, or pieces Grace and Ollie wanted to keep or give to people close to their father.

"Yeah. Dad left the house to us both, and the mortgage is fully paid off from life insurance. I'll still stay in the dorms during the week until I graduate at the end of this semester, but I'll come back here on the weekends. I figured Ollie would want to sell, but she was happy for me to keep staying here as long as I wanted. I think the village charm is rubbing off on her."

Ruth smiled, but inside her gut twisted a little. Things had been great between her and Ollie over the past few days. They had talked so much, and Ollie had really opened up about how things had gone with her dad toward the end, and about working through stuff around her feelings with her mom. She had even told Ruth about a great therapist she'd found who did virtual appointments that she was starting next week. There was one topic they hadn't discussed, though, and that was what happened next.

Once they were finished packing all of this up, Ollie would be leaving to go back to her life in the city. She had a job there, an apartment, and friends. A life outside of Wicker Hill and Ruth. Although it was only a couple of hours' drive away, the prospect made Ruth nervous. Of course, Ollie would come and visit Grace, and Ruth could go and visit her. They'd make it work, they had to somehow, because Ruth couldn't imagine Ollie walking out of her life for good. That potential was no longer an option. But now that she'd gotten used to Ollie being up so close, it would be that much harder to go back to text messages and phone calls.

"What about you, are you planning to stay in Wicker Hill now or go back to the city?" Grace asked as Ruth gnawed at her lip. She had considered moving back to the city to be near Ollie. But being back in Wicker Hill the past few weeks had reminded her why she loved this place, and it wasn't simply down to the comfort of familiarity. Sure, part of her return had been due to anxiety, but mostly she missed Wicker Hill and everything it meant to her. Her people were here, her life was here, her home was here. And Ruth worried that losing all of that again would lead to resentment. The last thing she wanted was to start her life with Ollie in that way.

"I'm sticking around here. City life wasn't for me, I'm a small-town gal through and through," Ruth said.

Ollie walked in and set bags of food on the table as Ruth glanced up. She wasn't sure what Ollie had heard or if it were her imagination, but the smile Ollie shot her way looked a little forced. The conversation needed to happen sooner rather than later, and Ruth promised herself she would broach it that night. They'd already discussed Ruth staying over, so there would be ample opportunity for a serious conversation. No matter what the outcome, Ruth knew they would make it work.

"Can I talk to you quickly?" Ollie asked as they were

finishing their food. Ruth nodded and followed her out to the living room for privacy.

"I know we had plans for tonight, but I'm going to have to take a rain check if that's okay," Ollie said, and there was a nervous energy to her movements.

"Is everything okay?" Ruth asked as she pushed down her disappointment.

"Yeah, something has just come up that I need to take care of ASAP. I'll be leaving soon to drive home. I should be back in a couple of days at the most. I'm meeting with the solicitor again to finalize everything at the end of the week, and I can explain it all then."

Ruth's heart dropped into her stomach. So much for their conversation, or all the time they had to figure things out. Ollie was going home and would only be coming back to complete paperwork. It was all happening too fast, and Ruth couldn't catch up with the time she'd thought she had as it slipped away. Ruth nodded as Ollie placed a soft kiss on her forehead.

"I promise I'll explain when I get back and we'll talk. I'm not running away, okay?"

Ruth smiled at the reassurance. She appreciated that Ollie understood she needed it. But she couldn't shake the feeling that this was going to be their life now. Making it work around stolen days together in between real-world monotony. As Ollie left to pack a bag for her trip, Ruth said her goodbyes to Grace and Sophie. Sophie knew her well enough to give her a concerned look. Ruth reassured her that she was looking forward to an early night and left to make the short walk home.

Ollie would be back in a couple of days, and they would talk. A couple of hours' distance in the short term was nothing if it meant keeping Ollie in her life. And if it came down to it in the long run, Ruth was sure there were ways to find compromise. Even if that meant moving to a suburb outside the city. The thought of leaving Wicker Hill again brought a pang of sadness to her chest as she walked through the main street she knew so well.

Ruth walked the scenic route and took in the place she loved more than she ever would have thought possible when she first arrived two decades ago. Her thoughts flicked to Ollie, and Ruth knew the same could be said for her, too. Wicker Hill was home, but so was Ollie. That was something Ruth became more and more sure of every day.

❖

Olivia turned the car up the dirt path and her heart began to beat quicker as she took in the cottage ahead. It really did look like something from a fairy tale. Olivia's palms were sweating with nerves as she switched off the engine. She sat for a moment staring at the door to work up the courage to walk through it. On the other side of that door was the woman who had upended her life in so many wonderful ways, and somehow managed to make it feel steadier than it ever had before.

Olivia had promised Ruth, what seemed like a lifetime ago now, when she had begun the journey that brought her to Wicker Hill, that she would make sure to create fairy-tale moments for them. As Olivia gripped the envelope in her hand and walked on shaky legs toward the cottage, she hoped this would be one to add to that already growing list.

Ruth threw the door open and had her arms around Olivia before Olivia had a chance to knock. She laughed at the enthusiastic greeting as Piglet jumped at her leg while they hugged tightly.

"Miss me that much?" Olivia asked as Ruth pulled back.

"Yes, yes, I did. Don't leave again, okay?" Ruth said jokingly as her cheeks tinged pink.

"Well, that's sort of what I've been working on," Olivia said, as she followed Ruth into the cottage. Piglet strutted into the room again, likely headed for her bed, but Ruth stopped and spun around with a furrowed brow.

"Wh-what do you mean?" The words were spoken with such a cautiously hopeful voice that Olivia wanted to wrap Ruth up and promise her all the fairy tales in the world. Instead, she held out the envelope and Ruth took it. Ruth opened the envelope and pulled out the now worn sheet of paper as Olivia's hands shook with nerves.

"Oh my God," Ruth said before she placed a hand over her mouth in shock. Tears sprang to Ruth's eyes as Olivia moved beside her. She took in the familiar image of two stick figures standing with the LEGO brick house between them and the childish scrawl of *Livy and Roo* beneath them.

"You kept this? I can't believe it," Ruth whispered softly as she traced her fingers across the drawing.

"I did. I couldn't ever bring myself to get rid of it. The little girl who drew it for me made me feel seen and heard, and well…important, at a time when I needed it more than ever."

Ruth turned to look at her and Olivia wiped a stray tear from her cheek as she cupped Ruth's face.

"And that little girl grew up to be the woman who made me feel all those same things exactly when I needed them most. See, Ruth, we've been an important part of each other's stories for far longer than either of us knew. And I know exactly how I want my story to end. Here, with you. Happily ever after. We deserve our fairy tale, darling."

Olivia leaned in and captured Ruth's lips in a deep, passionate kiss that left them both catching their breath.

"But your job, your home…" Ruth stuttered, clearly still in shock. Olivia led her to the couch, and they sat as she took the drawing and laid it on the table in front of them.

"Home is more than a lonely apartment in a city. I moved there to run away from my past. I don't want to keep running from things anymore, Ruth. I can move into my dad's place, well my place now, with Grace, and we can take this as fast or as slow as you're comfortable with. But you are my home."

Ruth smiled in disbelief as she wiped at her eyes with a small laugh. Her face sobered a little and she bit her bottom lip in what Olivia now knew to be an anxious habit.

"I want you here, more than anything. But I also know how things went before. You said yourself, you slotted into your ex's life, and she gave up nothing for you. I don't want to be that person. I want to stay here, but I want to be with you more. We can figure it out. But your needs are important, Ollie. I can't ask you to move to Wicker Hill for me."

Olivia took Ruth's hand in hers and stroked it softly.

"This is nothing like what I had before. The fact that you're even worried about that proves it. I know my needs are important. That's why I'm doing what I need and moving here for me. Because I don't want to be hours away from you waiting for the next time I get to see you. Grace is here, too, which is a bonus. My friends are only a couple of hours away, and they will be more than happy to host us when we want to visit. They all know how important following one's heart is, Ruth, and they've all found their happily-ever-afters from doing so. It's my turn."

Olivia wiped a tear from Ruth's cheek as her hopeful smile bloomed once more.

"Plus, this strange little village has grown on me. Dr Hegarty offered me a job the first time he found out I was a nurse, which naturally I scoffed at. However, he was more than willing to extend that offer again when I popped by there before leaving a couple of days ago."

Ruth shook her head and laughed. "I can't believe you did all of this."

"I wanted to make sure I had it all sorted before I spoke to you. And I knew I had to do it right away or I wouldn't be able to contain myself from telling you that I love you, Ruth. I love you and I want to spend the rest of my life adding to that fairy-tale list I promised you."

Ruth kissed her again, over and over, before pulling back and holding her face gently.

"I love you, too, Olivia. You're amazing."

Olivia jumped up and Ruth pouted before saying, "I want more kisses."

"I just have one more thing. Hold tight."

Olivia ran out to her car and grabbed the bag from the store she had stopped in on the way. Ruth had a dreamy look on her face when Olivia returned, as if she couldn't quite believe it was all real.

"I got this for us," Olivia said as she pulled the box of LEGO from the bag with a smile. Ruth laughed and shook her head as she looked between the box of colourful bricks and Olivia.

"We never got to finish our LEGO house. But better late than never, right?" Olivia asked with a sheepish grin.

"You really meant it when you said you'd fill my fairy-tale moments list, didn't you?" Ruth asked as Olivia set the box on the table and Ruth walked toward her. Ruth wrapped her arms around Olivia's shoulders and leaned up to kiss her.

"I told you I keep my promises, darling. And I meant it."

As she stood there in the fairy-tale cottage, kissing Ruth with every ounce of passion she contained, Olivia knew she was truly home.

EPILOGUE

"Why do you guys just kiss all the time?"

Ruth laughed against Ollie's lips before she turned to face the nine-year-old rolling his eyes at them.

"Because kissing is fun, Fin. Except for you. Not for at least another ten years," Ollie replied.

Finley rolled his eyes again as Ruth ruffled his hair.

"He gets that from you," Sam said pointedly to her wife Brooke. "She always rolls her eyes at me," she explained to the rest of the group as Brooke proved her point with an eye roll. It did bear an uncanny resemblance to her son's.

"You always make me roll my eyes," Brooke shot back with a grin, before she leaned in to place a quick kiss on Sam's lips.

"See, this is what I mean. My moms kiss *all the time*. All you guys do. I'm out of here."

The rest of the group laughed as Finley vacated his seat to walk over to the arcade machines.

Ruth glanced around the table and marvelled at the fact that only two years ago she didn't know any of these women well. Of all of the many wonderful things Ollie had brought to her life, these people were top of the list.

"I can't believe we're all actually here at the same time," Sam said.

It was a rare event that got them all to Blaze together. The first time Ollie had brought Ruth up to visit, Ruth had quickly understood why she spoke so highly of the bar. Ruth wasn't a big drinker, so the idea of hanging out in a bar during the day had never appealed to her. But the first time Ruth walked into this place with Ollie, she got it.

It was a relaxed, bright, and open space. Not only was it an inclusive queer place, it was also welcoming to parents, which wasn't something Ruth saw often in bars. It was equipped with pool tables and arcade machines and had stacks of board games to keep kids and adults alike entertained. Ruth could see why it was an easy choice for their group and their ever growing families.

"Auntie Roo, Auntie Roo."

Ruth turned her head to smile down at the child tugging on her pants leg. "Yes, Isla?"

"Baby?" Isla pointed at Ruth's stomach with a quizzical look. Ruth laughed at the scepticism on the two-year-old's face as she nodded.

"She doesn't believe me, so I told her to ask you."

Ruth smiled up at Finley, who had made his way back to the table to roll his eyes at his sister in the typical big brother way.

"Yes, sweetheart, there's a baby in here," Ruth said.

"How?" Isla asked with a serious look on her face.

"I'm tagging you in here," Ruth said to Ollie as the rest of the group chuckled. Isla looked between them as Ollie's cheeks grew pink.

"Sam, your kid needs you," Ollie yelled across the table. Isla frowned at the still unanswered question and toddled her way over to her parents.

"Chicken," Ruth murmured under her breath as Ollie shrugged sheepishly.

"You realize you won't get out of the conversation so quickly with this one, right?" Ruth nodded to her swollen stomach and Ollie scrunched up her nose.

"I forgot part of the whole parenting thing means I actually have to explain stuff to the kid. Can we outsource that part?" Ollie asked.

"That's what cool aunts are for, right?" Sam said as she winked at her sister, Lexi. Isla had gotten distracted on her way to her parents and hopped into Lexi's lap instead.

"Cool aunt status is firmly where we are staying," Lexi said in a singsong baby voice as she indicated between herself and her partner, Robyn.

"The only things you get to outsource to us are too much ice cream and fun day trips. We babysit, too. But the birds and the bees stuff is all on you, my friend," Robyn said as she gave Ollie a faux sympathetic smile.

"Speaking of ice cream, did you really have to get one this big?" Dani asked as she pointed toward the toddler in her wife's lap who was intent on devouring a giant bowl of ice cream topped with chocolate sauce.

"Yes, yes, I did. Didn't I, Maxi?"

Robyn cooed at Dani and Ruby's foster son as he gave her the biggest smile with his ice cream covered mouth.

"You can be the one to come put him to bed later, too," Dani grumbled.

They bantered back and forth for a while and Ruth sat back to take it all in. She watched Dani and Ruby fussing over Max as Lexi bounced Isla on her lap. Finley was cuddled between his moms laughing at something Sam said while Brooke gazed at them lovingly. It made her heart so full to know that her kid would see this multitude of ways to be a family.

Ruth turned to see Ollie watching her with adoration written all over her face.

"You doing okay?" Ollie leaned in to whisper in her ear. The action sent shivers down Ruth's spine, and she sighed in appreciation. She had still not gotten used to the way her body responded to Ollie so immediately.

"More than okay. I'm happy," Ruth said with a smile that Ollie returned.

"Do you want to ask her now?" Ollie said with a nod toward Robyn, who was sitting on the other side of Ruth.

It wasn't long after meeting Ollie's friends the first time, when it became apparent that Ruth and Ollie weren't the only ones with a shared past. Robyn was a firefighter, and had followed in the footsteps of her father, Declan. Robyn had lost her father to a house fire when she was a kid. Before losing his life, though, he'd managed to save the life of a little girl.

"You're looking at me weird," Robyn said as she turned to face them.

Ruth bit her lip as Ollie tapped her fingers against Ruth's hand. She was grateful for the grounding it provided.

"We wanted to ask you something," Ollie said, and Ruth was even more grateful to her for always knowing what to say. Ruth wasn't sure she could muster the right words, or any words for that matter.

"This sounds serious. Are you okay?" Robyn reached out to Ruth with concern in her eyes, and Ruth was so thankful to whatever powers in the universe had brought them into each other's lives. She had often wondered about the man who'd saved her and given his life trying to save her parents. Ruth didn't have to wonder anymore as she looked into the eyes of this woman, Robyn, whom she now knew to be his mirror image in not only looks, but in bravery and compassion.

"Declyn," Ruth uttered the name as Robyn tilted her head, not any less confused than before.

"What Ruth is trying to say is, we'd like to know if you'd

be okay if we named the baby Declyn. After your father," Ollie said.

Ruth's eyes filled with tears as Robyn stared between them in disbelief.

"Wow. That's…wow," Robyn said as the rest of the table seemed to tune into the conversation all at once.

"Who made Robyn cry? Robyn's not a crier," Sam stage whispered as Ruth chuckled and Robyn wiped at her eyes.

"I am not crying," Robyn said. Lexi, who had been close enough to hear the conversation in its entirety, placed a hand on Robyn's shoulder.

"You totally are, baby. Just own it."

Ruth stared at Robyn nervously as she smiled and let the tears slide down her cheeks.

"Obviously, it's a yes. I just can't believe you'd do that," Robyn said. Ruth heard murmurs between the group as Lexi filled them in on what they were talking about.

"I wouldn't be here if it weren't for him. Neither would this baby. That's something I want to honour," Ruth said with a sniff. She looked around to see there wasn't a dry eye at the table as they all raised a glass to toast the many things they had to celebrate.

"To happily-ever-afters!"

Ruth joined in with the chorus of cheers that came from around her and smiled at the soft kiss Ollie placed on her head. She turned her face up to meet Ollie's lips with her own and sighed. Happily ever after, indeed.

About the Author

J.J. Hale has been devouring books since she was able to hold one and has dreamt about publishing romance novels with queer leading ladies since she discovered such a thing existed, in her late teens. The last few years have been filled with embracing and understanding her neurodiversity, which has expanded the dream to include representing kick-ass queer, neurodivergent women who find their happily ever afters.

Jess lives in the south of Ireland, and when she's not daydreaming, she works in technology, plays with LEGO, and (according to the kids) fixes things.

Books Available From Bold Strokes Books

All This Time by Sage Donnell. Erin and Jodi share a complicated past, but a very different present. Will they ever be able to make a future together work? (978-1-63679-622-2)

Crossing Bridges by Chelsey Lynford. When a one-night stand between a snowboard instructor and a business executive becomes more, one has to overcome her past, while the other must let go of her planned future. (978-1-63679-646-8)

Dancing Toward Stardust by Julia Underwood. Age has nothing to do with becoming the person you were meant to be, taking a chance, and finding love. (978-1-63679-588-1)

Evacuation to Love by CA Popovich. As a hurricane rips through Florida, so too are Joanne and Shanna's lives upended. It'll take a force of nature to show them the love it takes to rebuild. (978-1-63679-493-8)

Lean in to Love by Catherine Lane. Will badly behaving celebrities, erotic sex tapes, and steamy scandals prevent Rory and Ellis from leaning in to love? (978-1-63679-582-9)

The Romance Lovers Book Club by MA Binfield and Toni Logan. After their book club reads a romance about an American tourist falling in love with an English princess, Harper and her best friend, Alice, book an impulsive trip to London hoping they'll both fall for the women of their dreams. (978-1-63679-501-0)

Searching for Someday by Renee Roman. For loner Rayne Thomas, her only goal for working out is to build her confidence, but Maggie Flanders has another idea, and neither is prepared for the outcome. (978-1-63679-568-3)

Truly Home by J.J. Hale. Ruth and Olivia discover home is more than a four-letter word. (978-1-63679-579-9)

View from the Top by Morgan Adams. When it comes to love, sometimes the higher you climb, the harder you fall. (978-1-63679-604-8)

Blood Rage by Illeandra Young. A stolen artifact, a family in the dark, an entire city on edge. Can SPEAR agent Danika Karson juggle all three over a weekend with the "in-laws" while an unknown, malevolent entity lies in wait upon her very skin? (978-1-63679-539-3)

Ghost Town by R.E. Ward. Blair Wyndon and Leif Henderson are set to prove ghosts exist when the mystery suddenly turns deadly. Someone or something else is in Masonville, and if they don't find a way to escape, they might never leave. (978-1-63679-523-2)

Good Christian Girls by Elizabeth Bradshaw. In this heartfelt coming of age lesbian romance, Lacey and Jo help each other untangle who they are from who everyone says they're supposed to be. (978-1-63679-555-3)

Guide Us Home by CF Frizzell and Jesse J. Thoma. When acquisition of an abandoned lighthouse pits ambitious competitors Nancy and Sam against each other, it takes a WWII tale of two brave women to make them see the light. (978-1-63679-533-1)

Lost Harbor by Kimberly Cooper Griffin. For Alice and Bridget's love to survive, they must find a way to reconcile the most important passions in their lives—devotion to the church and each other. (978-1-63679-463-1)

Never a Bridesmaid by Spencer Greene. As her sister's wedding gets closer, Jessica finds that her hatred for the maid of honor is a bit more complicated than she thought. Could it be something more than hatred? (978-1-63679-559-1)

The Rewind by Nicole Stiling. For police detective Cami Lyons and crime reporter Alicia Flynn, some choices break hearts. Others leave a body count. (978-1-63679-572-0)

Turning Point by Cathy Dunnell. When Asha and her former high school bully Jody struggle to deny their growing attraction, can they move forward without going back? (978-1-63679-549-2)

When Tomorrow Comes by D. Jackson Leigh. Teague Maxwell, convinced she will die before she turns 41, hires animal rescue owner Baye Cobb to rehome her extensive menagerie. (978-1-63679-557-7)